Prime Time Murder

Hollywood Whodunit 1

A Humorous Cozy Mystery

Brittany E. Brinegar

Contents

Book List

HOLLYWOOD WHODUNiT

0   Lake Day Shenanigans

1   Prime Time Murder

2   Stand-In Murder

3   Music City Murder

4   Trap Door Murder

5   Fool's Gold Murder

6   Holly Jolly Murder

7   Blue Suede Murder

Robinson Family Detective Agency

1   Red Herrings & Pink Flamingos

2   McGuffins & Birdies

3   A Hoax & a Hex

4   A Patsy & a Pastry

5   A Trick & a Pony

6   A Masterpiece & a Murder

Spies of Texas

1   Enigma of Lake Falls

2   Undercover Pursuit

3   Cloak & Danger

Prequel Offer

Curious how Becky ended up in Hollywood?

DOWNLOAD
THE FREE SHORT STORY TODAY!
www.brittanybrinegar.com/subscribe

1

Murder on the Set

I moved to California with a clear set of goals. Find an agent. Land a television show. Become a star actress. Easy peasy.

I sashayed into the studio for my first day unable to hide my excitement. I flashed my official all-access pass at the gym rat security guard, the girl operating the taco truck, and anyone who glanced my way. Today I didn't sneak on the lot. I belonged.

A coffee cup wobbled as I struggled to grip the door handle to the sound stage. I maneuvered the carrying tray to my hip and slid a sneaker through the cracked opening.

"Come on. I got you now." The thick metal door inched. I tucked a paper sack of breakfast goodies under my chin to free my other hand.

An assistant in a headset bustled outside, smacking me in the nose. Bagels spilled and rolled across the gravel walkway. "Awesome job, Coffee Girl."

I chased the runaways and blew off the dirt. "Three-second rule?"

The assistant claimed an espresso and studied the order taped to my bag. "Your delivery is to Studio 12, *Prime Suspect*. This is 3."

"Oops." I lifted my shoulders. "Luckily, no one saw the bagel incident."

He slurped from the Styrofoam cup.

I eyed the name on the label. "You don't look like a Sally."

"Nope. Thanks for the coffee. You saved me a trip." He grabbed the drink carrier and slapped money into my hand.

The friendly fellow danced inside the sound stage. I unfolded a wrinkled Lincoln. "Five bucks? This doesn't cover the barista's tip."

I returned to the coffee cart and started from scratch. When I pictured the glamour of Hollywood, I envisioned more screen time and fewer errands. But I agreed to pay my dues. At least the role of gopher got me near a television show. Acting adjacent.

Stars always told interesting stories about catching their big breaks at the mall or walking their dogs. Or how building cabinets led to a little space smuggler part known as Han Solo.

My mouth twisted as I imagined my discovery. Upon delivering the coffee, I say something witty and the director overhears, recognizing my irresistible charm.

I collected my order and abandoned the daydream. Maybe something witty will pop into my mind tomorrow.

With a better grip on my delivery, I asked for directions to Studio 12. A creepy, one-armed clown sent me down the wrong path. Shocker.

Lost with chilling coffee, I locked eyes with a security guard. When he ignored my existence, I whistled. "Excuse me, can you point me in the right direction?"

"I don't work here."

Fooled by another costume.

I wandered for a few minutes until I found the trailers for *Prime Suspect*. The streaming television show entered a second season despite dipping ratings. The serial format followed a single crime for the full run. The first year ended on a cliffhanger with the killer in handcuffs. Thin evidence, shoddy police work, and a questionable confession hinted to an acquittal in the near future. During the summer hiatus, rumors spread leaking problems between the cast.

I entered through a side door without incident. Darkness greeted me. Roll call said 8:30. In my excitement, I arrived hours before schedule. For those who knew me, arriving anywhere on time required a minor miracle. Early necessitated divine intervention.

My body continued to operate on Texas time, despite a month in the sunshine state...

"No that's Florida. What's California?" I tilted my head unsure of their nickname.

I squinted through the darkness and shuffled my feet. If I managed to reach my back pocket, I could flip on my iPhone flashlight. The tray wobbled but I held strong.

Sets, dressing rooms, and offices crowded the structure. A labyrinth of Hollywood magic. The cardboard backing stamped the set with an expiration date. I opened a door and entered the gritty New York squad room. Despite the crunch for time, I placed the tray on a teetering stack of books, propped my feet on a detective desk, and snapped a selfie. My friends back home would freak.

I pocketed my phone and returned to the director's bay. My eyes blinked at movement in the distance. "Is someone there?"

Out of nowhere, a hooded figure barreled into me. Coffee flew into the air as I slid across the slick, tiled floor. Hot liquid covered my jeans.

"Hey, watch out!"

Footsteps faded and a sliver of light spilled into the studio as the door burst open. A scruffy dog whizzed by, barking at the shadow's heels. I scrambled for my phone and activated the flashlight. Coffee and bagels littered the floor in a soggy mess.

"First day on the set. Nice work, Becky. You're sure to be fired now."

I scanned the darkness for a broom closet. A quick mop and another stop to the snack cart and problem solved. My clumsy adventures would remain my little secret.

I traveled through the bullpen to the interrogation room. On the other side of the door, I entered the lead character's living room. I froze at the scene.

A woman sprawled on the floor. Ghost white. If I interrupted filming I was fired for sure.

No cameras. No stage lights. I edged closer. The makeup department did wonders. Eerie. She resembled a real murder victim.

"Excuse me?" Recognition fluttered. Why did the star of the show, the accused killer, wallow on the floor in a pool of fake blood? "Maria Sinclair?"

I kicked at the bottom of her red sole shoe. No response. "Yup. I'm so fired."

2

Witness or Suspect?

I dialed 911 as I searched for a pulse. Flipping my phone to speaker mode, I described Maria Sinclair's condition to the operator. Within minutes, paramedics arrived and pushed me aside.

They pronounced her dead and radioed for the police department. I endured endless questioning from uniformed officers, detectives, and finally the agent in charge.

A short, red-haired man flashed a badge. "Agent Cornwallis, CBI. You the girl who, ah, found the body?"

"CBI?"

"California Bureau of Investigation."

My mouth tilted. "Did you bring Patrick Jane with you?"

"Who?"

"The fake psychic from *The Mentalist*?" I swallowed at the detective's lack of humor and my inappropriate timing. Switching tactics, I lowered my vocal pitch to cop-speak. "Yes, I discovered Miss Sinclair upon arrival this morning."

The agent unbuttoned his blazer and shoved a hand in his pocket. "You work on the show?"

"Sort of. Today's my first day on the set."

"Really?" A smile formed. "Actor, writer?"

"Aspiring actress."

"I'm a screenwriter." Cornwallis bounced on the balls of his feet. "On the side I mean. I'm pitching this pilot about an everyday working stiff who falls headlong into a drug-smuggling ring..."

A uniform officer cleared his throat. "Agent Cornwallis, you told me to tell you when the cast arrived."

"Yeah, yeah. Let me finish with the witness." He tapped his notepad. "So, you discovered Miss Sinclair around 7:30? Did you notice anything odd or suspicious?"

"A hooded figure bumped into me, spilling my coffee everywhere." I waved a hand over my caramel-coated clothing. "Oh, and a dog barked too."

"Did you get a look at the guy?"

"Between the hood and the darkness, no." I tiptoed and displayed the suspect's height. "At least five-foot-nine. I can't say if it was a man or a woman."

When you clocked in at five-feet-zero, everyone over the age of thirteen towered over you like a giant.

"After the suspect knocked into you, what happened?"

"I found the body."

"How well did you know Miss Sinclair?"

"I watched her on the show, but I never met her."

Cornwallis' brow twitched. "I thought you act on *Prime Suspect*."

I snorted. "No, sir. I'm an assistant."

He closed his notebook and stuffed it in his pocket. "That's all for now, Miss Roberson."

"Robinson," I corrected. "Becky Robinson."

"We'll call you with any more questions." He signaled to an officer. "You said the victim's boyfriend works here?"

"The ex-boyfriend." The officer lowered his voice. "Apparently, there was trouble in paradise."

My ears perked at the gossip. I didn't follow tabloid news but my roommate kept me updated on the juiciest tidbits. Maria Sinclair dated co-star Justin Woods for the last six months. Did a nasty breakup make him the prime suspect?

The cops drifted out of earshot and the associate producer snuck up behind me. I muffled a yelp. "Sorry, I'm jumpy."

"What do you think you're doing?" Extras, stand-ins, and other menial roles referred to Sherry Newton as the dragon lady. As fire spewed from her mouth, I couldn't disagree. "Why are you standing around?"

"The police interviewed me."

She spread her arms. "I don't see them now, do you?" The sugary Georgia accent warred with her biting tone. "We pay you to do a job. We fall behind and the show loses money."

"The star actress is dead."

"And you won't be taking her place. So how does your job change?" A jet-black eyebrow arched. "It doesn't. When filming resumes, the staff should be ready. A meeting is starting down the hall. If you want a second day on the set, you should probably hurry."

My sneakers stuck to the floor with every step. The sticky coffee spill left a trail of residue wherever I wandered. I entered the meeting and smoothed frazzled hair. I spent three days picking out my outfit, like a kid starting a new school year. Despite the careful planning, my first impression to my colleagues said, klutzy errand girl.

An hour after quitting time, I strolled through my apartment and tossed the keys in our designated bowl. "L.A. traffic is no joke."

My roommate wandered by the door, phone pressed to her ear. "No, Ma. Becky is the one with a job on *Prime Suspect*, not me. I'm not an actress."

I waved, passing along a signal to say hi to her mom. I crashed on the hand-me-down couch, too tired to change my clothes.

Lois sunk into the recliner drained from the conversation. "My mother is telling everyone who will listen, I got a role on *Prime Suspect*. Which isn't remotely true. I hate talking in front of crowds. I would be the worst possible actress. I'm a director... of sorts."

"What about me? Did you explain I'm only a coffee girl?"

"Next time." She waved. "How was your first day?"

I cocked my head. "You didn't hear yet?"

"No? How would I?"

"Well, about what you might expect. I got coffee for the assistant's assistant. I spilled a bag of bagels. Some guy in a headset stole my order. I found a dead body. Spilled coffee all over myself..."

"Wait, back up. You what?"

"Spilled. Everywhere. I smell like caramel."

"Hilarious, Beckers. Did you find a body? Like a prop?"

"A real, formerly alive person. Police are tight-lipped which obviously means homicide."

"Hold on while I grab the popcorn. This is juicy." Lois tossed long black hair over her shoulder. "And tragic. I probably shouldn't be so excited by a murder."

"Don't worry, just another box checked on your psycho-evaluation."

"Moving past my horror, fill me in. Who was murdered? Who did it? What was the motive?"

"Well, as is the case on every cop show, we solved the crime at the scene where the killer confessed and detailed their entire plan. Like a Scooby-Doo villain."

"I can Google the incident if you fail to take this seriously."

I hugged the pillow on my lap. "Maria Sinclair."

"No." Lois gasped. "I could see it."

"What?"

"Someone murdering Maria Sinclair."

"Why? She's a fan favorite. They decided to bring her back for the second season, despite ending her story."

"Yeah, fans loved her. But I heard the cast couldn't stand her. She demanded a bump in salary and control over her character arc. She told a gossip magazine *Prime Suspect* is doomed without her."

"Flimsy motive."

"People kill for much less."

"I overheard a cop mention she and Justin Woods split."

Lois slapped her armrest. "I'm so jealous. You always luck out with the best jobs."

"I wouldn't call what I'm doing glamorous."

"You are in the middle of a Hollywood whodunit. A true-crime story. You are a fly on the wall for the investigation. What more could you want?"

"I'm not sure the series will continue. I might be out of a job by Monday."

"What makes you think so? Not to say people are cold, but the show goes on if the studio can make money. This kind of press is ratings gold."

"Half the crew quit today."

"Why?"

"I guess they saw the whole murder thing as scary."

"Whimps." Lois leaped from her chair. "Does this mean there's a job opening? I'll do anything. You can put in a good word."

I twisted my mouth. "About you? Let me think. You're a hoarder who spills your collections throughout the apartment. You don't cook. You steal my chips, no matter where I hide them..."

"You're listing roommate problems. I do have some positive traits too."

"Which are?"

"Well, you know. I aspire to direct one day. Any job in showbiz helps." Lois possessed many admirable qualities, including humility which prevented her from ever bragging about herself.

"I'll talk to the associate producer on your behalf."

"Thank you." She hugged my neck.

"Fair warning, Sherry hates me."

"Why?"

"She either suspects me of the murder or she despises everyone."

"Gosh, I didn't even ask. You didn't do it, did you?"

"What can I say, I had a busy morning." I pinched my chin. "Who do you suspect? Based on the incredibly reliable gossip chain you subscribe to?"

"The Hollywood Hunk."

"What a cheesy nickname."

Lois dropped beside me on the couch. "Did you meet him yet?"

"Justin Woods? No."

"He spent most of season one in a supporting role. This year his storyline involves promotion to detective. He's getting a lot more buzz, on the cusp of stardom."

"So, he murders his ex-girlfriend who hogged screen time?"

"One of the many possibilities." Lois rotated her shoulders. "This is why you need me on set."

"You think we can solve this before the police?"

"Hello? You were a detective in your hometown."

I rolled my eyes. "My friends and I played detective as teenagers. Huge difference."

"You playacted quite well. How many bad guys did you put behind bars?"

My mind flickered to the past. "Enough. But I played a minor character in their story. The twins are the real investigators of the group."

"Okay, Eeyore. I'm solving this case with or without you." Lois grinned. "After you get me the job, of course."

3

Backlot Shenanigans

I fumbled for my house key as my phone buzzed in my pocket. Balancing a bag of groceries, I spilled into the apartment. I missed the table by the door and one of the bags crashed to the ground. Two Gala apples rolled across the hardwood but I answered in the nick of time. "Hello?"

"Becky, it's your favorite grandfather calling."

"Papa Beau! How are you?"

"Fine. Enduring your mother's cooking most nights when my stomach doesn't object." The soft Texas accent soothed and reminded me of home. "How's life in Hollyweird?"

I smiled at the crack. "Eventful."

"I only visited once for a rodeo. They rigged the broncs for the hometown boys. The only time I ever got seriously injured during a ride. You couldn't drag me back with the promise of a million bucks."

Beaumont Parker was pure Texas cowboy from his Resistol hat to his Justin boots. He hit the circuits at seventeen and never looked back. Not until the wear and tear of his body caught up to him.

"It's not so bad, Papa. And if you want to catch my face on the movie screen, this is the place I need to be."

"They're lucky to have your pretty face on loan." He added the last part, so I remembered California couldn't keep me. "How's your new job on my favorite show going?"

My pulse thumped. If my family, my mother mainly, learned about the murder, she might drag me home. "Fine and dandy. I took a selfie on the set. Perched at a desk in the squad room with my best stern cop face."

"This I need to see."

I laughed. "Sure. I'll send it to you later."

"Seen any stars yet?"

"One." Did a dead body count?

"Anyone I might know? Keep in mind all these new actors run together and don't interest me much."

"Um. I'm not sure you've heard of her."

"What are you hiding? I can hear something funny in your voice."

Papa Beau moved in with us after some health problems and my parent's divorce. As a young girl, I snuck into his room to borrow his rodeo buckles. Despite the large quantity, he always spotted one missing.

I sucked in a breath. "Someone on the set was murdered."

"Who? Someone in the cast?"

"Maria Sinclair."

"No kiddin'? Scuttlebutt is she might return for another season. The cops catch the guy yet?"

"I don't think so."

"Why are you sounding so uninterested? You always loved a mystery. Or have you forgotten old Lake Falls already?"

I curled my hair around my finger. "I'm interested. But I can't go snooping around the crime scene because I'm curious."

"Says who?"

"Papa! Are you trying to get me in trouble? Cops tend to frown on civilians butting into police investigations."

"What happened to those friends of yours? The ones you ran around playing detective with?"

"We grew up and went our separate ways. And *playing* detective is the key phrase."

"Oh, boy. You solved some humdingers." He whistled. "Crime-fighting is in your blood. My daddy Bo told some mind-blowing stories. He's a man who garnered respect everywhere he went."

"About his time in the Navy?"

"Those are interesting too. But his best tales came from sometime after. One day I'll tell you more." He released his belly laugh. "Call it an incentive for you to visit."

"I don't need a bribe, Papa Beau. I plan to come home often."

"So, you gonna dig into this murder?"

"Maybe."

"That's a yes. I can already tell you're hooked." The TV in the background clicked off. "Your mother's car pulled into the garage. Gotta go and pretend like I'm taking the afternoon nap she insists I need."

"Talk to you soon, Papa."

I arrived for my second day on the set with fewer nerves. After what happened in my debut, nothing could shake me. The phrase 'it can only go up from here' rattled in my mind.

On take two, I enjoyed my stroll through the iconic studio gate. An entire outdoor area was constructed to resemble New York City. A few blocks later, I entered downtown Chicago. A hop, skip, and a jump hurled me back in time to the old west. The lot amazed me and I contemplated hopping on a guided tour.

As the tethered golf cart whizzed by, I waved like a real movie star. The tourists oohed and aahed as they snapped my picture. Whispers asked my identity. Their guesses intrigued me. The prevailing answer seemed to be one of the Emma actresses.

I attempted a wink and a pose. My luck, the photographer caught me in the perfect millisecond to morph my face into a Frankenstein monster.

A movie shoot on a neighboring street drew my attention. A stunt man dangled from a building and dove to the mattress below. The actor popped into the frame, dusting off his jacket and reloading his weapon.

Despite the murder on the lot the previous day, the cameras continued to roll. While the *Prime Suspect* cast took a few days to mourn, writers retooled the script and Sherry ordered the crew to return. As I wandered the grounds, I ran through my spiel on why she should hire Lois, hoping I wouldn't squash my friend's chances.

A dog barked inside an old west saloon. A familiar yelp. I maneuvered my Ray-Ban look-alikes to the top of my head as I entered. "Here, doggy? Are you in here?" I peered around a corner, checking for rolling cameras. The last thing I needed was to interrupt filming. "Puppy?"

A bark and a whimper answered.

I dug through my messenger bag for a peanut butter granola bar. I tore into the package and broke off a corner. "Come here, puppy. I got a yummy treat."

The dog edged from the shadows. A loveable, shaggy creature. Folded ears with brown and white coloring. A spot covered the left eye. An adorable Jack Russell Terrier.

I tossed a tiny piece of the goodie and created a trail back to me. "This worked in Hansel and Gretel. But don't worry, I'm not a witch." I demonstrated my lack of powers with a Samantha Stevens nose twitch, a Jeanie arm fold, and a Sabrina point. None of which activated supernatural abilities.

One at a time, the pup nibbled the trail. I extended my hand with the last piece and rubbed behind velvet ears. "What a sweet girl." I checked for a collar. "What's your name? Are you a show dog?"

She slurped the peanut butter wrapper, requesting more.

"Sit. Roll over. Shake." No command prompted a response. "So probably not an actor." I stroked her back and ran my hands through coarse fur. As she grew accustomed to me, she licked my hand. "You look like the pup who flew by me the other day. Are you a witness to Maria Sinclair's murder?"

Red stained the dog's paws. "Perhaps more than a witness, Spot?" She frowned at the name.

"Okay, you're right too generic. I'll keep thinking. In the meantime, I need to call you something better than 'dog'. Any suggestions?"

I dug into my pocket and snapped a picture of the dog and the potential blood on her paws. "Let's find Agent Cornwallis. He might be interested in meeting you." Her ears perked. "Don't worry, I won't let anything happen to you. We'll find your family. I'm sure a cutie pie like you is chipped."

I patted my hip to test if she would follow. A wag of her dipped tail said she might. "There's more peanut butter where that came from, okay?"

I opened the saloon door and the terrier bolted. "Hey! We made a deal."

I raced behind her, kicking up dust on the wild west street. With ears flapping in the breeze, she hit the New York pavement at record speed. By the time I reached Brooklyn, she vanished. Shielding my eyes from the sun, I scanned the lot.

My watch buzzed with a five-minute warning alarm. If I arrived late for the staff meeting, Sherry would freak. "You and me ain't done, Cutie Pie. I'll be back."

Like a galloping horse, I dashed for Studio 12. On my way, I threw a shoe and ate pavement. "Real smooth, Becky." I massaged the rip in my straight leg jeans, hoping the hole looked like the expensive, premade variety. Bouncing barefoot, I searched for the strewn ballet flat.

"This yours?" asked a man in a Dodgers baseball cap and sunglasses.

"Yeah, I'm a regular Cinderella." I ceased the ridiculous hopping and touched my foot to the flaming blacktop.

"What did you hit, a moving truck?" He closed the gap and displayed my shoe. The material gashed down the center as if it passed through a shredder.

I shoved my toes into the ruined footwear. "Where's a cobbler when you need one?" I wouldn't make five feet with a flopping flat.

"You might try Festus, the Best Ye Olde Shoemaker in Dodge City."

"A. Festus is a deputy on *Gunsmoke*. B. I just came from the old west and found a ghost town."

He snapped his fingers. "Thought I might sneak it by you. Not many people catch a *Gunsmoke* reference anymore."

"My grandpa lived with us growing up. Satellite TV features a channel running *Gunsmoke* and *Bonanza* all day long. I caught all 600 episodes. Twice."

He laughed and pointed to my shoe. "I'm no cobbler but I think I can help. What size are you?"

"I wear a... sev... eight... and a half." I grimaced. "Spare me the snickering. I never grew into my feet. Eight is an average women's shoe size. Not considered big feet if I wasn't vertically challenged."

"I didn't say a word." His eyebrows twitched. "Give me a minute and I'll try to find you something to wear. I think I saw a clown dressing room around here somewhere."

"Funny."

The mysterious stranger returned a few minutes later with sneakers dangling over his shoulder by the string. "I couldn't find any clown shoes but I did locate these."

"Perfect. Thank you."

"I figured sneakers are the safest choice. I bring you the six-inch heels and I'm looking at a lawsuit for reckless endangerment."

I double-knotted the laces. "Thanks for the help, Prince Charming." I coughed. "You know, from the Cinderella story because I lost my flat and she forgot her glass slipper. I can't imagine how she continued with one shoe, hurry or not."

He chuckled and touched a hand to his baseball cap. "You're welcome."

I backed away and checked my watch. I was way past the time of turning into a pumpkin.

I entered the meeting and my mind fixated on the encounter with the mysterious blonde stranger. As an aspiring actress, you'd think I could dial down the dorky factor on command. If I ever found the off switch for my awkward trait, I'd be thrilled.

Sneaking through the door, I slipped into an open seat. I craned my neck to read my neighbor's handout.

Sherry Newton shoved glasses to the tip of her nose. "The producers want me to mention the availability of a therapist. If any of you people who never met Maria Sinclair feel concerned enough to share your emotions with a professional, the option is available to you. Although, I would think colleagues and friends might take precedent, so expect to wait in line."

Agent Cornwallis entered the conference room. "We're ready for the interviews."

"Ah. Already? This the government is early for." Sherry consulted the time on her phone. "Well, apparently the CBI has questions for you people that can't delay any longer. Detective, Agent, what do we call you?"

"Agent Cornwallis." He clapped his hands. "Afternoon, folks. I consider myself a member of showbiz so I understand the pressures of your jobs. Miss Sinclair had many comrades on the set and I hope some of you can shed light on her situation."

A girl next to me snickered to a buddy. "She controlled minions not friends."

A hipster with glasses and a beard raised his hands. "Did the coroner rule on COD yet?"

The agent blinked. "COD?"

"Cause of death." The hipster stroked his beanie. "Don't you cops use acronyms."

"Only on TV, pal." Cornwallis adjusted a polyester necktie. "We haven't ruled out any possibility. This is early in the investigation."

Another hand raised. "Is it true Ashton Ashley is the lead suspect?"

The actress with two first names was a new addition to the cast. She and Sinclair engaged in an infamous Twitter feud but recently mended their relationship. Some suspected only for the good of the show.

"Ah, this, ah, isn't a Q&A, folks. I'm supposed to be the one asking the questions." He handed a stack of business cards to the front row. "Hand those out, would ya. Each of yous take my card.

Call the office if you think of anything useful. Did you spot anyone suspicious yesterday morning? Did anybody hang out around Miss Sinclair's dressing room..."

"They're looking for suspects. She was totally murdered," the loudmouth next to me said.

"Now, now don't start a rumor. We didn't announce anything official." Cornwallis smoothed thinning red hair. "All I'm asking is for information, so we can determine what happened yesterday."

As the meeting dispersed, I hung back to speak with the agent. "Excuse me?"

"Roberson, you got anything new for me?"

"Robinson. Remember how I mentioned a bark before I found the body."

"Not specifically but I'm sure I made a note."

"I bumped into her on another set."

He scratched above his eyebrow. "Who?"

"The dog. A Jack Russell Terrier." I flashed the photograph. "She hid inside an old west saloon. I wanted to bring her back with me but she took off." I zoomed. "I think she has blood on her feet."

"I doubt it. No paw prints near the body."

"Shouldn't we find her? Maybe she witnessed the murder."

The agent scoffed. "She's a dog. Do you expect her to bark at the killer and point him out in a lineup? Come on."

Did I Bugs Bunny the agent into confirming a homicide?

"So, you have no interest in her?"

"None."

"Alrighty." The next time I found Cutie Pie, my duty wouldn't be to the investigation.

With the meeting concluded, I flagged down Sherry. "Mrs. Newton, can you spare a moment?"

"You arrive late and now value more of my time? Obtain the homework assignment from a classmate."

"I apologize for my tardiness but this is regarding another matter."

"Proceed." She flipped raven hair over her shoulder.

"If the staff is still short-handed, I can recommend someone for a job. She's hardworking and detail-oriented."

"By all means. We should put you in charge of all hiring and firing decisions." She removed a compact from her purse and reapplied lipstick. The shade complimented her dark skin tone. Despite her angry disposition I had to admit, the woman possessed impeccable style.

Did everyone in Hollywood make better fashion choices than me? "I don't think I'm boss material. People tend to walk all over me when I'm in charge."

"Color me shocked." Sherry marched down the hall, dismissing our conversation.

I jogged to catch her. "Can I tell her yes?"

"Did my answer sound like a go-ahead?"

"If I act dense and say yes, will I increase her odds?"

"Is she as annoying as you?"

"Definitely not. Lois is a stickler for time. If the invitation says 6:00 she's at the party before the caterers."

A slight exaggeration since neither Lois nor I ever went to parties. But the statement held true. My roommate loathed my lack of punctuality.

Sherry's mouth pursed. "College kids and rabid fans are knocking down our door to land the most menial job on our set. We're a hot ticket item. Why should your friend warrant special treatment?"

"Do you want annoying students taking selfies at the crime scene and posting them on Instagram? Anyone you hire now is chasing the publicity."

"Hmm."

"What?"

Her brow furrowed. "I'm surprised. I hate you slightly less than I did five minutes ago." She swiveled on a killer heel. "Tell your friend to report to HR bright and early in the morn. What's her name?"

"Lois Vo."

I skipped from the studio and dialed her number. News this exciting shouldn't be delivered via text message.

4

Forensic Evidence

Lois pounded on my bedroom door. "I'm leaving without you in five minutes."

I changed my outfit for the third time. A floral sundress, matching magenta sweater, and Keds. "No, you aren't. Today is my turn with the car. You're stuck with me."

"Becky, we can't be late on my first day. I want to make a strong impression on the dragon lady."

"Here's a tip, be sure to call her by the nickname. She's famous for a superb sense of humor."

"I'm almost certain you're giving me bad advice."

I swung open my door. "Very perceptive, Lo."

"Why did you change so many times today?" Her eyebrows rose. "Any charming reason in particular?"

My mind fluttered to the *Gunsmoke* fan who I might never see again. Me and my big mouth insisted on sharing the embarrassing encounter. "You're reaching, Lois. Hanging around glamorous Hollywood types all day makes a girl self-conscious about her wardrobe."

"You're fine, let's go."

"I spend an hour getting ready for fine?"

Lois slapped her forehead. "You forgot the infliction."

"Whatever, I'm not changing again. This is as good as it's going to get."

I glanced around the stained walls of our tiny apartment in the sketchy part of town. Half of our belongings remained in boxes as if we expected to run home at any minute. We hung our Texas A&M

degrees side-by-side on the plain back wall with senior pictures. The extent of decorations. The place could use some sprucing to provide a homey touch.

I longed for a leading role and a Beverly Hills address. When Lois directed a blockbuster sensation with me as the lead, perhaps we could afford the astronomical property prices.

"Did you know Ashton Ashley is organizing a vigil tonight for Maria Sinclair?"

"Interesting how feuds are dissolved postmortem." I bustled into the kitchen for a breakfast bar.

"They patched their problems before casting Ashton on the show," Lois explained. "Although at the time, Maria's role consisted of a small appearance in the second season to resolve her story."

"What are you hinting at?"

"Well, Ashton portrays the friendly, grateful, childhood star part to a tee. Underneath, she's catty."

"Phony." I chomped into a Gala apple. "So, you think they postponed the Twitter war while the show transitioned to a new lead character?"

"Basically."

"But fans didn't want Maria Sinclair to leave."

Lois snapped her fingers. "Jealousy is a compelling motive."

"This analysis is unrelated to your hatred of Ashton Ashley?"

"She ruined the last season of an iconic sitcom. Brought on to replace the aging children with a cute six-year-old."

"She's cousin Oliver."

"You need to update your references."

"*Brady Bunch* is timeless." I tapped the pockets of my sweater and rifled through my purse. "Whoops."

"What now?"

"I can't find my badge."

"You lost it already?" Lois dropped on the sofa. "Excuse me a moment while I slowly die of stress."

"Relax. I forgot it yesterday and the guard at the gate took pity on me."

"No wonder murderers are flitting all over the studio."

"He remembered me from my first day. Hard to forget the gal who discovered a body." I dumped the contents of my purse. "Whelp, I guess I'll bite the bullet and request a replacement."

"Awesome idea. Can we leave now?"

"Let's go, pilgrim."

"I'm reporting to human resources first, you know. The longer you take, the worse impression I make."

I swung open the door to find Agent Cornwallis, his hand poised in the knocking position.

"Gee whiz." I clutched my heart.

"Miss Roberson, can I ask you a few questions?"

"Robinson. I'm on my way to work. I can't be late three days in a row."

"This won't take long."

The satchel dropped from Lois' shoulder. "I'm dead meat."

I tossed her the car keys. "Go on ahead. If you speed and run every light, you'll make it with time to spare." I eyed the cop. "Any chance on a police escort?"

Cornwallis stepped aside for Lois to pass. "I'll pretend I didn't hear your suggestion." He unbuttoned his bargain-basement suit and entered the living room. "Nice place."

"Came with its own ghost, so we got a bargain on the rent."

He flipped through the pages of his notebook and clicked a blue pen. "I wanted to clarify a few things with you. As the investigation progresses, new things come up, you understand?"

"Sure. Can I offer you a cup of coffee?"

"Milk and sugar."

I bustled into the kitchen and tapped the button on the instant machine. I leaned across the island and poked my head through the cutout. "Shoot."

He spun on the couch. "I prefer your undivided attention where we can look each other in the eye."

"You sound like every teacher I ever had." Coffee percolated at an agonizing drip. "This visit sounds different from our previous chats."

He tapped his nose. "Right you are. Perhaps you might take this seriously. I don't want to haul you to the station, but I will."

"Can you answer one thing for me, Agent?"

"Fine."

"Why is a CBI investigator working the death of a movie star? Isn't the LAPD equipped to handle homicide?"

"The attorney general's office will request our presence where they deem necessary. Including the sensitive investigation of public figures." He cleared his throat. "Coffee is ready."

I plucked mismatched mugs from the cabinet and filled mine with half milk. I wanted to be a java fan like my hero Lorelai Gilmore but the beverage curled my nose. The cup sloshed on the table as I passed it the Cornwallis.

He sipped and mopped the spill with his tie. "You described someone fleeing the crime scene and bumping you. A few minutes later, you discovered Miss Sinclair."

"Yes."

"Did you move the body?"

"I checked for her pulse. When I didn't feel one, I called 911."

"Did you touch anything else on the set?"

"Probably?" I lifted my shoulders. "I know enough about cop shows so I tried to avoid contaminating the scene. Other than touching her neck and wrist, I'm not sure."

"Did you at any point flip the body?"

"That I would remember."

"Interesting."

My brow furrowed. "How so?"

"From the time you discovered Miss Sinclair to when the first responders arrived, did you leave the immediate area of the body?"

"No." I blinked. "Yes. I left for maybe thirty seconds when I heard the paramedics. I found them at the front of the sound stage and led them to the set."

"You provided exemplar fingerprints so the crime lab could rule you out?"

"The first officers on the scene suggested I do so to help the investigation." My posture straightened. "You're not looking at me as a suspect, are you?"

"Too early to say, Miss Roberson. We are in the process of collecting evidence and running down every lead."

My heart thumped. They couldn't think I killed her? I reported the body! Moisture wicked my palms. If they arrested me, I would need a lawyer I couldn't afford. Or worse, forced to call my mother. Though she mostly handled property law in our small hometown, she worked criminal before I was born. The thought of confessing my faux pas made me sick to my stomach. Even as a witness, she would lecture me for not calling her at the scene. Mix-ups happened every day.

"Should I repeat the question?" Cornwallis asked.

"Yes. Sorry."

"Did you interact with the victim?"

"I told you before, we never met."

"Technology is a fascinating thing." Cornwallis scrolled through his phone. "Twenty years ago, few places used functioning security cameras. Those who did, well the picture looked like one of them Picasso paintings. Today everywhere is in the range of a camera. Whether hidden or someone's selfie stick, someone is always watching."

"Creepy. Sounds like a fantastic plot for a movie. *Persons of Interest* started with the premise but it became too confusing for me to follow. Which is saying something."

"Well anyways, technology in some ways is making a criminal's job easier. But our crime lab is keeping pace." He turned his phone. "The tech guys sent me this photo from the night before Maria Sinclair's death." He pinched the screen. "This angry girl in the background looked familiar to me. I racked my brain, wondering who she resembled. Then it hit me. You."

"Me?" I choked on my coffee. "She's out of focus, but I assure you she is not me."

"Where were you three nights ago?"

"Home binging *The Office*."

"You conjured your alibi mighty quick."

"I'm always home binging *The Office*. I reach *Goodbye Michael* and fully intend to watch the Robert California torture years, but *Diversity Day* pulls me back to season one."

"What are you babbling about? Alibi or not?"

"Alibi. Lois can confirm."

"Who?"

"My roommate who you met earlier."

"The Chinese woman?"

"Vietnamese." I studied the picture and scoffed at the resemblance. "Your girl here is wearing 600-dollar stiletto heels and a barbed-wire tattoo." I shoved the sleeves of my sweater. "No ink on me."

His forehead creased. "People pay that much for ugly shoes?"

"And they aren't comfortable."

He scratched his head. "At a couple of dollars a pop to produce they must make out like bandits."

I stood and smoothed my cotton dress. "If we are done, I should hurry to the set."

"Not quite. Say it's not you in the picture. We still uncovered evidence at the scene we can't explain."

"Which is?"

"I'm not at liberty. The forensic experts assure me the clues we found couldn't be lost while you checked the body. You dropped something and the victim bled out on top of the item."

"You're kidding? I didn't lose anything."

"Bloody fingerprints don't lie."

My throat tightened. "Are you arresting me?"

Cornwallis stood and smoothed his tie. "Not at this time. We are continuing to collect evidence."

"Why would I kill someone, report the crime, and wait around for the cops?"

"So you could use the ridiculousness as a defense."

"Brilliant. You discovered my sinister reverse psychology plan."

"People say sarcasm is a form of a guilty conscience."

"Stu..." I bit my tongue. "You can address any further questions to my lawyers at Pearson Specter Litt." The reference to a fictional law firm brought a smile to my tense face.

"Very well."

I locked the door behind Agent Cornwallis and sighed. How did I find myself in such a ridiculous situation? If not so serious I might laugh. I couldn't be a legitimate suspect because of flimsy circumstantial evidence. What did they find to implicate me?

I focused on the memory, wondering what I left behind. I carried my messenger bag the first day loaded with twenty pounds of stuff I didn't need. Any number of things could be lost and I'd never notice.

I gasped. My missing security badge.

If they found an ID card with my name, picture, and fingerprints in the victim's blood, underneath the body... I might suspect me too.

Setting my jaw, I jumped to the most logical conclusion. I needed to catch the real killer before the coppers fitted me for my orange jumpsuit.

5

Officers Robinson and Vo

The city bus bounced along a crowded L.A. street as I formulated a plan of attack. Somehow, I would clear my name from the suspect list. I channeled Rick Castle and asked what he would do in a similar situation.

I scratched the analogy. Castle benefited from resources, connections on the force. Me, not so much. To uncover information, I engaged my creative side.

As I entered the studio, I remained at square one. Too many questions about Sinclair's murder made it impossible to start an investigation. Cause of death? Who had a motive? Opportunity?

What if she wasn't murdered?

Cornwallis all but confirmed foul play in his interrogation. Returning to the Castle analogy, I mapped an outline.

1. Body Discovered
2. Investigate Crime Scene
3. Medical Examiner
4. Talk to Next of Kin
5. Deep in Thought Reflect at Murder Board
6. Crazy Castle Theory
7. Interview First Suspect
8. Alibi
9. Dive into Personal Life of Victim
10. Discover Secret
11. Accuse the Wrong Person
12. Last Minute Ah-Ha Moment

13. Close Case and Banter with Beckett

A proven formula most procedural cop shows followed. Problem was, I found the body but I never investigated the crime scene. I acted as a witness and failed as a detective.

My first bout with murder knocked me off-kilter. Details from the scene fogged in my mind. I didn't remember losing my badge under the body.

I skipped to number three on my list – Medical Examiner. A plausible starting point. Getting them to talk to me? Another problem altogether.

Two laps through the sound stage and nearby trailers left me searching for my best friend. I fired another text to Lois, asking her whereabouts. If she didn't answer soon, I'd ping her location. Not an overreaction, given the killer-on-the-loose situation.

The soundstage door flung open. Lois power walked into the sunshine, her eyes focused on her task.

"How did your meeting with HR go?"

"Exciting." She slowed for my shorter legs to keep pace.

"Which of these things is not like the other – human resources, humorless, regulating, exciting?"

"I enjoyed myself. They gave me tons of handouts and a map."

"Ooh. A fold-up map of the studio? They don't give those to just anyone. You must earn the privilege."

"I think they come with every tour ticket. There's a stack of them in the office if you want me to snag you one."

I opened my mouth and popped it shut. "Please do."

"How did the interview with Cornwallis go?"

I cocked my head to the side. "You're looking at the number one suspect."

Lois tripped over a pebble. Funny how the klutzy people gravitated together. "What? How?"

"Seems my missing badge ended up under the body covered in my bloody fingerprints. For some whacky reason, they find that suspicious."

"Becky this is terrible. What are you going to do?"

"Wait patiently for the cops to clear me and find the real killer."

"Yeah. I'm sure. I see your mind turning. What's your plan?"

"Still percolating." I shoved a finger at her tote. "Where are you assigned?"

"Sherry called me a floater. I'll run errands between various departments while we are short-handed." She jiggled the bag. "Today I'm assisting in the wardrobe department."

"Ding. Coffee is ready." I wiggled my eyebrows.

"I don't like the sparkle in your hazel eyes. It means you concocted a scheme I'm going to hate."

"Spare the I'm not helping speech, Ethel. We both know you love my schemes."

"Ethel? I'm totally the Lucy of our dynamic duo."

"In your dreams."

"Tabling the argument. What's your idea?"

"First thing we need is reliable information. As of now, we're spewing potential killers like internet stalkers. To find credible suspects, we require cause and time of death."

"Now would be a splendid time for a friend on the police force. Doesn't the show employ consultants?"

"They don't converse with the likes of us." I snorted. "A set is worse than high school with cliques. The actors are the popular kids. The stuntmen are the jocks. The directors are the artsy types. Writers are the shy loners. The stand-ins are the teacher's pets, doing anything to call attention. Consultants are the brains. You and me, the assistants, are the bottom rung on the food chain. Below the band geeks. We are the invisible new kid who moved to town from one of the forgotten Midwest states."

"Wow. How long did you work on the analogy?"

I snapped my fingers. "Spur of the moment improv, thank you."

"Must I beg for your idea?" Lois shifted the tote to her other shoulder.

"Your placement today is fate. We'll need to borrow a couple of costumes."

"Day one and I'm already putting my dream job on the line."

"Doing laundry is far from your dream job. The overflowing hamper at home proves it." I opened the door to the wardrobe trailer. Another assistant bustled outside with an armful of clothes.

The clothing racks were organized by character. Justin Woods' outfits consisted of cool blue and green while the lead cop preferred earth tones. I parted the sea of cotton. The hanger scratched across the metal rod.

"What are you looking for?"

"My size."

"What's the name of the kid actor?"

I shoved Lois in the shoulder. "You're hilarious." I pulled an outfit from Ashton Ashley's section. More than ten inches taller than me and three sizes smaller. Who besides those in the entertainment world could maintain those proportions?

I migrated my search to the rack of extras' costumes. Police uniforms in all shapes and sizes greeted me. I passed a uniform to Lois and chose the shortest trousers for myself.

"What am I supposed to do with this?" Lois held the costume to her body.

"You wear it."

She rolled the clothes and tossed the hanger. "No way. Impersonating a cop is a crime. The fact you're facing a murder rap doesn't mean I want to tarnish my impeccable record."

"Not impersonating. Acting."

"And stealing."

"Borrowing. Your manning wardrobe today. Think of this as a field test of the costumes."

"You wear the uniform, I'll stand guard."

"As what, my witty consultant? We should play to our strengths, Lo."

"Aren't two officers a crowd?"

"Partners legitimize our cover." I stretched for a patrolmen's hat on the shelf. "You wanted excitement. Live a little."

"I meant gossip at the water cooler. And Twitter investigations. Not active crime-solving."

"Next time be more specific."

I stepped into the polyester pants. Why did they choose authentic, stuffy material? I belted the trousers and cuffed the dragging legs with safety pins. As I tucked in the shirt, I shined the shield pinned to my chest – NYPD. Perhaps the ME's office wouldn't notice we represented the wrong coast.

After logging less than ten minutes on the lot, we snuck off to our car. Lois drove while I provided directions to the Los Angeles County Medical Examiner's building.

Lois swiped sweaty palms on her pants. "This is going to blow up in our faces."

"Act the part and no one will question our belonging." I adjusted my hat. "We are police officers seeking the truth. Project confidence and let me do the talking."

The blue uniform provided an all-access pass inside. We bypassed security and followed the signs to the ME's office. A helpful receptionist directed us to the coroner handling the Maria Sinclair case.

"Shouldn't this building be more secure?" Lois whispered.

"Why must you question our good fortune?"

"If we can sneak in without trouble, why didn't the press?"

"We're savvier." I pushed through a cold metal door and tucked my cap under my arm. "Dr. Eklund?"

A headlamp shined in my eyes. "Yes?"

Lois puckered her cheeks. "Oh, gosh. What is that smell?"

The doctor adjusted a sheet. "First autopsy, Officer?"

Lois retreated through the door, in search of fresh air or a wastebasket. And then there was one. I clicked my black boots together. "Rookies."

Dr. Eklund paced to a desk and retrieved his phone. "Janet paged me. You say Agent Cornwallis sent you?"

"He requested we collect the report on Maria Sinclair."

"I uploaded the file to his office yesterday." The doctor snapped the band of his rubber glove.

"You know how these state agencies operate. The right-hand doesn't keep tabs on the left."

"Isn't that the truth? I'm sorry you wasted a trip." He pushed safety goggles by the bridge.

"No biggie. Sprung us from speed trap duty on San Bernardino." I hiked my utility belt and paced to the door.

"Tell your partner to bring a lozenge next time. The distraction and soothing peppermint help settle the stomach."

I spun on my heel. "Hey Doc, I hate to be a bother, but I'm thinking I should cover my bases here. Cornwallis and the CBI probably lost the paperwork and are gonna blame my department. The Sarge will give us a two-day rip for not following-up. Can you spare a minute to run through the file for my report?"

He stroked his stubbled chin. "Sure thing. Not like anyone is waiting for me when I get home tonight."

He slid a metal rolling stool to the computer. He shook the mouse, interrupting the county logo bouncing on the screen. A florist's website covered his web page.

"Getting a jump on Valentine's day? Some of these places take orders six months in advance."

He chuckled. "Worse. I'm in the doghouse with the wife."

I sucked in a breath. "What did you do, Eklund?"

"I'm not even sure." He spread his arms. "I missed the argument completely."

"Roses are a classic. Says I'm sorry for any husband's mistake."

"She will probably knock off points for creativity."

"When's her birthday?"

"April something."

"Something?"

"Cataloged on my phone with a reminder. I didn't miss it."

I suppressed a laugh as I Googled birth month flowers. "Daisy is her flower if you want to make a personal touch. She'll be impressed."

"Women have birth month flowers?"

"Men too. All you need to qualify is a birthday."

He typed 'daisy' in the search bar. "Twenty-three types of daisies?"

"I take it you aren't a botanist." I pointed to an arrangement. "Go with this one. The bigger ones say you're trying too hard."

He added the flowers to his cart. "Alright, Maria Sinclair." He clicked to a new window. "Cause of death: Blunt force trauma. Time of death: between four and seven. She bears defensive wounds on her arms and legs and we found skin cells under her fingernails."

"DNA match?"

"The lab is working on it. We'll know in a couple of weeks."

"Did you officially rule homicide?"

"Oh yes. She didn't bash herself in the noggin."

I scribbled in my notepad. "Any guess as to murder weapon?"

"Hard to say. Blunt instrument. Took several whacks to cause this kind of damage."

"The murderer likely showed signs of a struggle?"

"I say so. Messy, up-close, and personal crime."

"Which tells you something about the killer and victim relationship?"

Dr. Eklund held up his hands. "Woah, psych is way outside my area of expertise. Save the profiling for the pros. I simply read the evidence."

I slapped my notepad shut and tucked the pen in my shirt pocket. "Thanks for running through this again, Doc."

"No thank you." He tapped on the plastic frame of his outdated monitor. "Saved my bacon."

"Pick up her favorite dessert too. Ice cream, chocolate, or whatever."

"I should probably memorize that. Any chance they publish a birthday month cheat sheet?"

"You're on your own this time, Doc." I saluted and exited the autopsy room.

My iron stomach survived the Titan at Six Flags after two corny dogs and a grape soda. Nothing could defeat me, including a postmortem examination.

I padded down the tiled hall, in search of my best friend. I rounded a corner and bumped into Lois.

"Looky here." She shook a manila folder, gyrating so much I couldn't make out the contents.

"What am I supposed to see?"

"I photocopied the crime scene report."

"You what? How?"

"I sweet-talked the lab guy."

"No, really?"

"My queasy stomach brought me to an empty room with a stack of reports waiting to be logged. This one featured the handy 'Maria Sinclair' label."

"Excellent work, Ethel."

"This score should promote me to Lucy."

"Not when you hear what I found. I know who the killer is."

6

Meet and Greet

Okay, so maybe I didn't know who the killer was exactly. But Lois kinda stole my thunder popping in with the crime scene report. I had to say something to steal her spotlight. Not a complete lie since the autopsy at least provided me with suspects. One of which surely killed Maria.

From the safety of our car, we read the analysis. Fingerprints, fibers, unidentified particulates, all the buzzwords mentioned in CSI. In college, I took astronomy for my science credit. The reports were total gibberish.

"They found a shoeprint outside the studio." Lois handed me a photograph featuring squiggly shoe marks and a crime scene marker. "Lab tech didn't match the tread to a brand yet, but the size is a men's twelve."

"In blood?"

Lois squinted. "In mud."

"Not the smoking gun I hoped for. No telling the age of the muddy footprint." I flipped through the pages. "What else?"

"You and your ID badge are featured prominently."

"I figured. But I'm certain of my innocence." I blew stringy hair from my face. "We need a clue to push our investigation forward."

"Beckers, check out the catalog of her purse."

"Three hundred bucks in cash rules out a robbery."

"Specifically look at the keychain."

I traced the picture. "The cheesy couple's knickknack variety-." Maria Sinclair kept the locked heart half. The item sparked recognition. I thumbed through the photos and froze. Evidence marker seventeen framed the key to the heart. "Who carries both halves?"

Lois jabbed a finger at another photograph. "Dropped by the killer?"

"Rather convenient."

"Most murderers aren't rocket scientists." Lois clapped a hand over her mouth. "Do you realize what this means?"

"What?"

"Her boyfriend gave her the keychain."

"A likely scenario."

"And lost it while killing her."

"Perhaps."

"Becky, I think Justin Woods killed her. This is solid evidence."

"Or Maria's new boyfriend gave her the heart. She and the actor boy split weeks ago. Why would they keep the reminder?"

"One way to find out, we sneak a peek at Justin's keychain. This one in the photograph broke at the clasp."

I closed the file and put the car in gear. "We better hustle back to the set. We've been gone too long as it is."

"What are you supposed to be working on, anyway?"

"A lunch order. Uber Eats is delivering. I'll meet them at the gate and pretend like I ran the errand."

We changed out of our borrowed costumes and returned them to the wardrobe department before anyone noticed our absence. I parted ways with Lois and delivered food to my assigned area – props.

They supplied me with a new list of gopher duties as a mass text from Sherry popped on my screen. Staff meeting in one hour. I completed my assignments in record time. The menial activities flew by with my mind occupied elsewhere.

The evidence began to build against Justin Woods. Blunt force trauma said crime of passion. The broken keychain and men's shoe print further implicated the ex-boyfriend. But what about his motive?

I slipped inside the conference room and claimed the seat Lois saved. Sherry clomped to the front of the room followed by the cast. Since being hired, my only interaction with the stars came postmortem.

Dodger Boy, who rescued me from my footwear malfunction, entered last. What were the odds we worked on the same show? I hid a grin and elbowed Lois.

Her brows knit together and she tossed her shoulders.

The guy removed his cap and fluffed dark-blonde hair. I gasped, realization hitting me. Justin Woods was the *Gunsmoke* fan.

Lois smacked her forehead. "How does the self-proclaimed TV expert not recognize one of *Prime Suspect's* main characters?"

"He dressed like the Unabomber. How was I supposed to know?" I sunk into my chair and propped an arm on the table.

"Pipe down people." Sherry hammered a thermos on the front table like a gavel. "I can tell by your murmurs you recognized members of the cast. They are here for a specific announcement. So knock off the starstruck teenager bit and act professionally. Ashton Ashley, they are all ears."

"Thank you, Sherry. You are a rock during this difficult time." The actress tucked blonde hair behind her ear, flashing multiple piercings. "I want to start with a moment of silence for our friend and colleague, Maria Sinclair."

I peeked through my closed eye to scan the suspects... actors. Justin bowed his head and clutched his hat, playing the grief.

Ashton fidgeted with her ring and tapped her wedges. She concluded with the sign of the cross. "Thank you. Maria was a wonderful person and a rare talent. Those who knew her well are truly blessed. Though my addition to the show came during her final bow, I am lucky to walk the halls with her." She paced around the table and stalked the audience rows. "Many critics are concerned about our fate on *Prime Suspect*. Can we carry on without Maria? Should we? In my moment of crisis, I turned to my fans on social media. Thousands, nay, hundreds of thousands of people are reaching out with support for our television family. As a cast, we voted to continue with season two, retool, and honor Maria. Our wonderful writers are working overtime to craft the perfect story to explain the absence of Maria's character. And the producers agreed to post a remembrance at the end of the first episode. We believe it will make a beautiful tribute. What she would want. Do you guys have any questions for me?"

A guy in the brownnoser first row raised his hand. "We're stoked you joined the show, Ashton."

"Aw, thank you. I am overjoyed to join this family. I look forward to beginning this special season." She clutched her locket. "With everyone's help, we can make this year our best yet." She paced to the front and nudged Justin. "Say a few words."

"She's a tough act to follow. Inspiring speech." He cleared his throat and crossed his arms over a broad chest. "I'm sure the others up here will say lots about M.J., so I won't hog the floor. One thing I hope you keep in mind is privacy. Speculation is floating throughout social media and we don't want our own people talking to the press and fueling the fire. Let the police do their job and find the truth."

I studied the polarizing speeches. In context alone, Justin came off as cold and distant. His body language didn't do anything to assuage his guilt.

Ashton on the other hand said all the right things with a pasted-on, artificial smile.

But did either reaction make the actors viable suspects?

The star of the show, an aging movie actor grasping for a hit television gig, spoke next. Favoring the Allstate spokesman (President David Palmer from *24*), he provided an imposing presence in the interrogation room. In real life, a snoozefest reading off index cards. Talk about a letdown.

Sherry ushered the actors outside and turned her ire on us. "Nuh-uh. Sit down. We aren't concluding the meeting because the glee club left. This is where the actual work begins. I'm tired of the slacker approach from you people. Filming resumes in two days. It is our responsibility to make sure everything is ready."

"Mrs. Newton, don't forget about..."

"Shut up, Roger. I'm not finished." She cocked a hip. "Somebody, I don't know who, is leaking information to the press. Mr. Woods hinted at this but he is too polite to point fingers. If I catch any of you Tweeting, posting, Snapping, or Instagramming I'll fire you so fast your head will spin. Do your jobs and leave the gossip to TMZ and the police. *Prime Suspect* is on the verge of being canceled. One more incident and we're done for good."

Roger slid a folder across the table. "Mrs. Newton?"

"Oh yeah. One more announcement." Sherry unfolded reading glasses. "The studio is cutting back on funding, meaning no more new hires. Each of you people will be expected to do the job of two. Expect to cross areas. Every morning will present a new assignment." She crumpled the note. "Dismissed."

Lois covered her mouth and leaned into my ear. "I can't decide who I found more suspicious, Justin or Ashton."

"They're both winning." I tapped my fingers on the table. "If I intend to clear my name, we need to follow Justin."

7

Paparazzi

My eyes traveled over my best friend's ensemble. "What are you supposed to be?"

She lowered gigantic round sunglasses. "I'm incognito."

"As Jackie O?"

"This is Hollywood. Everyone dresses like this."

"They *did* in 1965."

"If we're stalking a movie star, I don't want to be recognized as an employee of the show."

I sunk lower in the driver's seat as Justin Woods exited the studio. He carried a gym bag and a motorcycle helmet. "Uh-oh. Our assignment became a tad more difficult."

"Why?" Lois removed the scarf from her head, producing static cling on her straight, black locks. "Motorcycle? Doesn't he know those things are dangerous?"

"He got his start as a stunt man. I'm more worried about losing him in traffic."

"Reading up on his IMDb page?"

"No." Yes.

The bike revved and Justin spun out of the lot. I put the Nissan 300ZX in gear, excited to test the new used car's limits.

Lois and I pooled our graduation money and splurged on the somewhat rare four-seater. Though any passenger riding in the back, would benefit from shorter legs.

The 1991 sports car predated our birth but we purchased the automobile for a song. The old lady who sold it to us in San Antonio only drove to and from work and logged less than 100,000 miles. We added more driving to California than she did in the last two years.

The red sportbike zipped to the boulevard, whizzing by palm trees. The area reminded me of every establishing shot when television shows visited Hollywood.

Lois yanked on her seat belt. "He's in an awful hurry."

"I wish we cloned his phone and tracked his GPS in case we lose him."

"You can do that?"

I twisted my mouth. "People on TV can. I cannot."

"So why bring it up if it isn't an option?" Lois huffed. "I should be driving, Grandma."

"This guy is flying as if contending in a motocross competition." I flicked my turn signal and shifted lanes. The car behind me honked, despite my 'thank you' wave. The bigger the city, the worse the drivers' manners.

I closed the gap, pushing further over the speed limit and jeopardizing my blemish-free driving record. We whipped in and out of traffic for ten minutes.

"Do you think he's going home?"

Lois glanced up from her phone. "Anybody's guess. You're the one with the bright idea to stalk him like paparazzi."

"How else are we supposed to dig up dirt on him?" Candy-apple--red flashed in my vision, exiting I10 to Bundy Drive. "I think we're driving toward the beach."

"Everywhere in L.A. is toward a beach." She pinched her phone screen, zooming in on the map. "Maybe he's surfing at Venice B-each."

"And his gear is where? Folded in his gym bag?"

"Shark tank idea, fold-up surfboard."

I scrunched my nose. "Back to the drawing board, Ben Franklin."

"Didn't we discuss modernizing your references? Ben Franklin practically predates the country."

"How about Thomas Edison?"

"Better. He at least made the 20th century."

The light turned red and I rolled to a stop behind the motorcycle. "What do you think his motive is?"

"A messy breakup?" Lois lifted her shoulders. "Too soon to speak in specifics."

Investigating was difficult enough with suspects and family members lying to the police. For newbie amateur detectives, near impossible. Every lead required legwork.

Justin whipped his bike to the curb and cut the engine. One benefit to his mode of transportation – easy parking.

"Open lot over here."

I flicked my blinker and froze. "Twenty dollars? No thank you."

"Beckers, all these lots are pricey close to the beach."

"Sounds to me like they're exploiting tourists."

"Well, duh."

"Between lot fees and gas prices, it might be cheaper to ride the bus."

"Park it. We're losing our suspect."

I fed money into a machine and received a ticket stub to place on my dash. Hardly official looking.

We darted across the lot and hit the sidewalk in a sprint. Lois leaned hands on her knees. "Hold on, I'm dying here."

"Push through to your second wind."

"Long gone. I'm on my fourth or fifth."

I dragged her forward by the arm. "Come on, Drama Queen."

"If you recall, I don't do well in the heat. The temperature is searing my skin."

With an eye roll, I returned my attention to relocating the movie star. When Justin came into view, we slowed our pace. He slung the gym bag over his shoulder and turned on the boardwalk. Tourists and locals crowded the area. Bicycles whizzed by followed by joggers and professional dog walkers. Keeping track of the actor in the masses took all our concentration.

"Good thing he's six-foot-two. He stands above most of these people."

I narrowed my gaze. "Now who's studying his IMDb page?"

"Only for research on the case. This infatuation is all yours."

"The murderer thing is kind of a turnoff."

"My, aren't you picky?" Lois shielded her eyes from the blinding sun. "Couldn't he travel somewhere with air conditioning?"

Though warm, the sunshine didn't melt my skin like back home. No matter how much Californians and Lois complained about the heat, nothing compared to the forty-five days of August in Texas.

My first trip to the boardwalk lulled me into a trance. A unique scene. I could only describe it as a hodgepodge of homemade products, entertainment, and exercise. A man in a Jamaican hat banged drums. A group of talented kids danced better than I knew possible. A couple with muscles on their muscles power walked by like instructors in a 90s fitness video. The dense population provided excellent cover until Justin turned into an alley behind a pizzeria.

"I think this is as far as we can go."

I peeked around the corner. Dead end. "You might be right."

The restaurant door swung open. A stocky man with a sauce-stained shirt waddled outside.

"What's going on?" Lois leaned beside me.

"I don't know, I can't hear anything."

"Don't you claim to be a proficient lip reader?"

"Not from this distance with their backs to me."

The stranger's appearance sent a shiver through my spine. Justin plowed a hand through his thick hair and paced. He folded his arms as he addressed the man.

The sloppy man stroked a pencil-thin mustache.

I squinted at his lips. "*Payment.*"

"What about it?" Lois asked.

The mouth garbled before I recognized another word. "*Quiet?*"

Justin fished in his gym bag for a roll of cash and slapped the money into the man's outstretched hand. The man licked his fingers and counted his compensation.

"What's going on now?" Lois peeked again.

"Hollywood made Mr. Pizzeria an offer he couldn't refuse."

"Blackmail?"

"Or payment for a hitman?" I scrambled against the brightly painted building. "Scram he's coming back."

Lois ducked into a tent offering street tattoos while I browsed a seashell accessory booth. I tried on a floppy hat as the actor passed. He retraced his steps down the boardwalk. I waited a minute before rejoining Lois, who scanned a sample booklet.

She looped her arm through mine with gaping eyes. "Good timing. I almost panicked and got inked."

"Your mom would kill you."

"What now? Do we follow Justin or his blackmailer?"

"We should give Corleone a wide berth. Let's find out if the actor scheduled any additional shady deals on his calendar."

We increased our pace and returned to our car.

"From paying off blackmail to an L.A. country club, sounds about right." I focused the dial on my fold-up binoculars. Justin and his motorcycle entered through the front gate of the Chalet on the Hills Country Club after scanning an ID badge.

"What's he doing now?" Lois reached for my binoculars.

"Driving through the security out of view."

"I guess this is the end of our stalking?"

"You would be wrong. I'll think of a way to gain access."

A quick Google search gave me insight into their visitor policies. They didn't offer tours and only allowed preapproved guests accompanied by members. I clicked on the membership tab. No dollar signs graced their pages. The subtext – if you must ask the price, you can't afford the fees.

The four-acre grounds included an eighteen-hole golf course, clubhouse, nine LED-lit tennis courts, a gym, both indoor and outdoor Olympic sized swimming pools, dining, and an event ballroom.

"This might be a waste of time." Lois drummed on the dash. "You want the inside scoop from the Chalet and to rub elbows with movie stars."

"An added benefit." I continued to scroll the webpage. "Country clubs breed gossip. They love sharing secrets and dishing on scandals."

"Secondhand rumors. They might not be familiar with the victim or Justin."

With a victorious flare, I displayed my phone. The social page of the Chalet featured an 'In Remembrance of Maria Sinclair a Valued Member and Friend'. "Care to adjust your position?"

"Okay, genius. How do we sneak inside?"

I started the engine and circled to the rear of the club. Following the signs to the service entrance, I ticked through a plan. "We can roam freely as the help."

"True but I'm sure security is tighter for employees."

I parked across from the employee gate and engaged my binoculars. A catering van labeled Cutsie Cupcakes rolled through to the tower. After exchanging paperwork, they received a keycard to scan. The gate buzzed and slid open. The van continued to the loading docks where a worker greeted them and signed for the boxes of catered treats.

A Jeep Wrangler entered next, loaded with three caddies. They followed a similar procedure to the cupcake delivery but the security guard never batted an eye at their presence. They each scanned cards and proceeded through the service door.

Two waitresses traveled from the nearby bus stop and strolled inside. The three methods represented potential covers. Which would suit us best?

"The evening shift is arriving now." I scrubbed my eyes and checked my watch. "No way around the need for a security badge."

"I can get us a badge."

"No, you can't."

Lois jiggled her eyebrows. "Want to bet?"

"How?"

"Now I'm the one with the secret plan. How's it feel, Ethel?"

"Cockiness isn't becoming, Lo."

"You're always cocky."

"Confident. Huge difference. How are we getting inside?"

"What's your knowledge of automobiles?"

"Non-existent."

"Excellent. This role shouldn't be a stretch." Lois flipped to an open page in her notebook and storyboarded her idea.

My clammy palms tightened on the steering wheel. With a deep breath, I entered the mind of my character. I winked at Lois, hidden in the bushes as I turned into the country club. I stopped at the gate and waved at the security guard inside the tower.

The window slid sideways and a young rent-a-cop twisted his face. "Yes?"

"Is this the entrance to Universal Studios?" I laid on a thick Texas accent. "I bought a ticket on the five o'clock movie star tour."

"No."

"Are you sure?" I opened my door and climbed out. The Z sputtered as I left the engine idling.

"Quite."

I leaned on the window with Lois' fold-up map and indicated his nametag. "Where are we at on here, Tarleton?"

He squinted his serious blue eyes. "This isn't even the right studio."

"It's not? Really?" I twisted the map. "Oops. My hotel supplies one of those walls of brochures and whatnot. No wonder I'm so lost. So, what's this place you're guarding? Does a movie star live here?"

"I'm going to have to ask you to turn around, ma'am. You're blocking the entrance."

"I will, I will. But can you maybe give me directions? I already drove in circles for hours."

"Not part of my job description. Google it."

"This is embarrassing, but I blew through all my data for the month during the Hollywood Walk of Fame tour."

Tarleton massaged the bridge of his nose and drew a smartphone from his utility belt. He rotated the screen. "Here's your route out of here."

"May I snap a pic of your screen?" I snagged his phone and backtracked to my car. She sputtered again and five minutes of idling led to one outcome. I only needed to delay a little while longer. I returned to his window with a lift of my shoulders. "Oops, I closed the map before I took the picture."

He tugged on his brown locks, spiking the hair even further. "You got to be kidding me." Another car pulled in behind mine. The guard waved for them to wait. "I'm sorry but you need to move your car. Park on the street, come back, and I'll try to help. But if traffic backs up, my boss will chew me out."

"I apologize, honey. I'll scoot out of the way in a jiffy." I jumped in my car and slammed the door. The Z chose the perfect time to abandon her old age quirks. I made a show of searching for something. With a sheepish smile, I crept back to the booth. "Forgot my phone."

He shielded his eyes and exited to direct traffic. He motioned for the car blocking me in to back up.

I slipped behind the wheel as the Z coughed. Dials raced. The engine stalled. I resisted the urge for a fist pump. My eyes landed on the rearview mirror as the guard approached. I turned the key, pleased with the clunky dead motor sound.

The guard's entire body slumped, jingling the keys on his belt. "What now?"

"Zelda is kinda finicky. She sometimes overheats and stalls."

"Pop the hood and I'll take a look."

"Ah, so sweet of you. Good thing you're handy with cars. I couldn't tell you the difference between a battery and the brake plugs."

He maneuvered to the front of the car and I popped the trunk. "No. The other one."

"Whoopsie. I got the right one now." I scratched my head and popped the gas tank.

He huffed and reached inside the car. "Right here." With hands on his hip, he studied the interior of the car. "I'm not seeing an obvious problem."

My eyes cut to the booth as Lois exited with a thumbs-up confirmation. "Sometimes Zelda needs a breather. Let me give her another try." The engine turned over and started.

Tarleton swiped his forehead with the sleeve of his black security jacket. "Finally."

"Thank you, I'll get out of your hair now." I waved as I backed to the street and met with Lois. She displayed two all-access badges and a beaming smile.

8

Country Club Charade

Fearful the rent-a-cop would recognize me, we stashed the car a block away and hiked to the employee entrance. I tied my long hair into a ponytail and added a sweater and sunglasses to my ensemble.

I cut my eyes to the booth as we scanned the cards reserved for the visiting help.

"The card doesn't work," Lois said through a cracked voice. "I messed up, Becky. These aren't active."

My security guard pal tapped the glass window. "Upside down, rotate it."

Like a deer caught in the middle of a highway as a truck barreled near, Lois froze. With my back to him, I spun her card and the gate buzzed a response. "Move it, Lo."

She released a breath. "That was close."

Her nervousness rubbed off on me as we stepped through the service entrance. Employees bustled back and forth like ants. My pulse hammered. I nudged my thumb to the women's locker room. Apparel with the Chalet logo would help us blend in.

I dressed in a baby-blue polo and golf shorts. Lois opted for black trousers, a crisp white shirt, and a vest – a staff uniform.

"Split up and speak to as many people as you can. If you find Justin, follow him."

Lois tilted her head. "How does one dig for information without sounding like a gossip seeker. I mean, why would anyone talk to a random waitress?"

"The method is different for every situation but generally, act uninterested in the details. You can't appear overeager. Casually mention Maria or Justin and go fishing. If you catch a nibble, drop another line and reel them in."

"You might not realize this but I am a terrible fisherman."

"You'll do fine. The staff will be more likely to talk to you while members are more apt to provide something relevant. Good luck."

I squeezed her shoulder and navigated the hallway.

After a scan of my ID, I entered the patron area. Prominent, preppy people roamed the grounds. I snagged a stack of towels and followed an older woman in a bathing cap to the indoor pool.

I edged beside the woman as humidity and chlorine invaded my senses. "Towel ma'am?"

"Yes, thank you." The woman draped the striped material over her shoulder.

"You're welcome." I touched her arm. "I love your shoes. They are so cute."

She wiggled her painted toes. "Aren't you sweet?"

"May I ask where you purchased them?"

She tapped fingers on her mouth. "I can't remember. I bought them years ago. Probably from a department store now out of business."

"Really? They reminded me of something Ashton Ashley wore on a magazine cover. You're setting a trend."

The older woman waved away my comment. "When you're as old as me, you live long enough to experience many trends come back into style."

"Perhaps I'm mistaken, I think Maria Sinclair is the actress sporting the sandals. Shame what happened to her."

"Oh, my yes."

"I saw her a few times around the club. I am a huge fan but I never approached her. I didn't want to be a bother. Celebrities come here to escape the hubbub."

"A smart decision. Maria earned a reputation for getting people who crossed her fired."

"You're kidding?"

"I don't want to speak ill of her but she was an odd one. Didn't care to participate in community events. Kept to herself."

"Based on the characters she played, I never pegged her as shy."

"Probably the wrong word." The woman's face pinched. "Some people called her stuck-up. She acted better than those of us not in the entertainment world. She labeled anyone who engaged with her as a crazed fan invading personal time."

"Something tells me most of y'all are immune to being starstruck."

"Honey, I met Jimmy Stewart and Clark Gable back in the day. The last people I'm impressed by are small-time method actors." She adjusted her cap. "I'm showing my age. Do you even know who those men are?"

"Of course."

"You don't have to humor me."

I cocked an eyebrow at the challenge. "*Rear Window. Anatomy of a Murder. Vertigo. The Man Who Shot Liberty Valence. Rope. The Man Who Knew Too Much. Gone with the Wind. Teacher's Pet. Misfits. It Happened One Night.*"

Her bottom lip dipped. "Possibly millennials aren't doomed after all."

"My Saturday nights are spent with Turner Classics."

"My kind of girl."

"Well, I'll leave you to your swim. Nice talking to you."

Despite my beginner's luck with the sweet older lady, my subsequent conversations smacked into dead ends. Several people appeared creeped out the help would engage them in conversation.

I moved my exploration outdoors. Bright sunshine blinded me for the first few moments. I debated my options – tennis courts, driving range, or the patio.

I plucked an outdoor umbrella and approached a group of young women. Each blonder than the next. They sported expensive diamonds and designer clothing. As I drew closer, I caught pieces of their conversation.

The platinum blonde ran fingers through her hair. "Allen is in the process of casting his new independent film. I thought about snatching the lead, but my schedule is quite busy and the shoot would clash with my guest spot on... the show which can't be named yet."

The other women cackled. The dirty blonde sipped a fruity drink. "I should audition."

"Honey, the role is a legitimate dramatic part. Not the slapstick you're known for."

"More serious than Allen's deodorant commercial with the kicking donkey?" the strawberry blonde asked.

Platinum reapplied lipstick. "One commercial doesn't mean my soon-to-be-ex-husband isn't an important director."

"But a slasher movie does?"

Dirty Blonde received a death glare from Platinum. "Says the wife of... oh I forgot, you're an old maid."

Strawberry crossed her legs. "You should be an expert on husbands. You are divorcing number three."

"Excuse me, stare much?" Platinum's dark false eyelashes fluttered as she scrutinized my presence.

The heavy umbrella clattered to the ground. I jumped to avoid smashing my toes. "Care for some shade?"

"We're working on our tans, something you should try." Platinum flicked me away with the back of her manicured hand.

"Sorry, I thought you might be talking about the movie Justin Woods is starring in."

"Starring?" Strawberry snarled. "He isn't much of a leading man type. He can't garner a storyline on his bottom feeder show."

"Now with Maria out of the picture, he can land some screen time," Dirty Blonde said.

"Not unless someone gives him acting lessons." Platinum coiffed her perfectly styled hair. The style resembled a movie star of the 1960s. "If the producers possess any smarts, Ashton will gain creative control and carry the load."

"Wow, y'all really don't like Justin."

Dirty Blonde puckered her lips and hissed. "Y'all? Did you recently hop off the bus from Arkansas?"

"You caught me. Why the hatred for Justin?"

"He's a whiny crybaby who demanded Maria not be brought back for a second season," Platinum said. "After she broke up with him, he couldn't deal. As if they were the first Hollywood breakup. Be mature. I handle my exes all the time."

Strawberry parted her hair with her sunglasses. "If working with exes was your hang-up, you couldn't work in the entire state of California."

The valley girl accents pierced into my brain, fogging my ability to think. "He wanted Maria gone?"

"Is she hard of hearing?" Strawberry asked.

"He threatened the studio behind her back. Said 'it's her or me'." Dirty Blonde pushed a piece of salad with her fork. "Honestly, not much of a threat. He's like the backup quarterback making demands to walk."

Platinum showed frown lines across perfect porcelain bronzed skin. "Since when do you understand football?"

"I played a cheerleader murder victim a couple of weeks ago. Some of the extras, college players, taught me."

I resisted an eye roll. I wanted to confirm the reliability of their account but I couldn't ask directly. "I heard a different story after their breakup."

"Where? Spying on people in the steam room?" Platinum flipped her hair. "I heard from my ex-husband's assistant's brother who is an extra on *Suspects.*"

"Oh, well. I didn't realize your husband's assistant had an inside man."

"Why are we talking to her?" Strawberry jiggled her empty drink. "I need a refill."

"I'm sure one of you knows a producer's second cousin's aunt who works here as a waitress. She can help you, I'm sure."

I missed the *Mean Girls* craze and only caught clips and GIFs of the movie. Something told me the blondies would fit right in.

I marched to the nine tennis courts on the east side of the grounds. My cell buzzed and I checked my text messages.

After sending the thumbs up emoji, I and entered the court. A tennis ball whizzed and pegged me in the rib cage. I doubled over and dropped my phone.

"Are you okay?"

I blew dust from my case. "Otter Box continues to be my best purchase."

"You shouldn't enter a live match with your nose in your cellphone."

I squinted at the tennis player dressed in all white. Justin Woods witnessed yet another clumsy moment.

"Where were you with the spectacular advice thirty seconds ago?"

He clicked the button to stop the ball machine. "Don't I know you?"

"We work on the same program. Well sort of. I'm not an actress or anything. I go on coffee runs and fetch props and take lunch orders."

He pointed. "Clown shoes."

At least I made an impression. "I'm silly for not recognizing you the other day. You're the lead actor on the show where I'm employed. Talk about embarrassing."

"Don't feel bad. No one ever recognizes me. I have one of those forgettable faces." He spun a tennis racket. "You work here too?"

"No." I glanced at the insignia on my polo. "Yes. This is a new job. Turns out working on a television set doesn't pay much."

"For a moment there, I thought I developed a new stalker."

I coughed. "What?"

"A joke. A bad one." He tugged on his visor. "I didn't see you at the staff meeting today."

"I was there. Ashton Ashley gave an empowering speech."

"Yeah. She did."

"Yours..."

"Terrible. I'm aware." He massaged the back of his neck. "I'm not skilled at public speaking and Ashton says all the right things."

An opening. I tamped down my excitement. "Sounds like you question her sincerity."

"She has many sides to her. All of which are opportunists."

"I gave her the benefit of the doubt. At least she and Maria put the feud nonsense behind them."

Justin huffed. "Like I said, skilled speaker."

"I find in public speaking, it helps to speak from the heart as Ashton did. You should open up next time."

His expression hardened. "I prefer to keep my personal life private."

"I can understand. But next to Ashton, you came off cold and callous. Maybe a smidge bitter?"

"Yeah. I hear the whispers."

"What whispers?"

"Don't play dumb. I realized why you're here, asking about Ashton and Maria. The same reason anyone talks to me these days. You want the inside scoop." The vein in his neck pulsed.

"People are curious. By not talking, you fuel the fire."

"How about my right to grieve in private?"

"You're in the public eye. People talk about the fights between you and Maria in the weeks leading to her death."

"We didn't fight. Contrary to popular belief, we split amicably."

"Unless they're told the story, people love to speculate."

"Are you the leak?" He took a step closer.

"What?"

He hovered over me. "Someone is selling information to the press. Is it you?"

I swallowed. "You sound paranoid."

"But you're avoiding the question."

"I might have a big mouth but I'm no gossip."

"I liked you better when you didn't recognize me."

"You're not the only one with a forgettable face. I'm the one who discovered the body."

"Becky Roberson?"

I threw my head. "Robinson."

"You found Maria?"

"I suppose my curiosity led me to snoop. I apologize for invading your privacy."

He scrubbed the light blonde stubble on his chin. "You're investigating?"

I muffled a snort-laugh. "I don't think you can compare my bumbling questions to any type of investigation. After my initial statement, the police shut me out. Quite different from TV. I envisioned myself as Patrick Jane... from *The Mentalist*."

"My first role was on the show as Teen at Crime Scene."

"No way. Which episode?"

"I'm not telling. I stumbled over one measly line. Thinking about my wooden performance still makes me cringe."

"Hey, I wish I could say Patrick Jane hypnotized me or I worked at CBI. At this rate, I'll never earn my own IMDb page."

"Nothing happens overnight. I'm still waiting for my big break. *Prime Suspect* is supposed to be my shot."

"Can I pretend to be a detective and ask you one question?"

His smile slipped. "No."

"One and I'll drop it."

"I highly doubt it."

"If you don't like the question, don't answer."

"How about I play you for it?" Justin pointed at the court.

"Tennis?"

"Naturally."

I rubbed my rib cage. "I'm already sporting one bruise from getting in the way of your fastball. Don't think I want another."

"Then you don't ask your question."

I chewed my lip, confused by his actions. I couldn't decide if the conversation made him more or less suspicious. I needed my one question.

"Fine. How do we play?"

"One round, no advantage."

I scrunched my nose. "I'm not sure what that means but I'm sure you'll keep the scoring honest."

He jogged to his bag and retrieved an extra racket. I gripped the 300-dollar Babalot, afraid I might drop or scratch it. I tossed a ball into the air and batted it into the net without zip or spin.

"I'll let you serve."

"What a gentleman."

My first and second serve found the bottom of the net. I switched to the other side and stretched my back.

"Love-Fifteen."

"What?"

"The score."

"Oh, yeah. Zero-One." I rocked on my heel and got my momentum. The serve shot over the net, hitting the corner of the box. Ace. "Back to even."

I buried the next offering at his feet. He sent a strong lefty forehand to the line. I lunged and swatted a two-handed backhand. The spin curved beyond his reach.

"15-30?"

"30-15, unfortunately."

From my favorite side, I smacked another Ace.

"45-15."

"40-15," he corrected.

"Why? I thought we counted by fifteens?"

He slung his racket over his shoulder. "Yeah, the scoring is strange."

"But one more and I win?"

"Just serve."

I retreated to my spot and blasted to the corner. Justin lunged and popped the ball high into the sky. I circled and lined up for a smash to his backhand side. Painting the line, I counted my chickens before they hatched. He picked up the short hop and fired a textbook backhand. I charged the net and pointed my hips to his right. He bit. With a flick of my wrist, I dropped the ball two feet over the net.

"60-15 or whatever makes game, McEnroe."

Justin hopped over the net. "Hey, you pulled my leg with those first few serves and not understanding how to score."

"Not at all. My serve is rusty and the scoring in tennis is stupid. My best friend played on her high school team. We play almost every evening and she is super competitive. I either got better or got killed."

"I'll say."

"So, about my question."

"I'm going to regret this." He rubbed his temple. "Go ahead."

"Can I inspect your keychain?"

"My what?"

"Whatever you keep your keys on. Can I see it?"

"Why?"

"I won the question, remember?"

Justin dug through his gym bag and handed me the ring. I inspected each one, not giving away what I searched for. I paused at a broken piece of metal. The jagged shard remained as if ripped from the ring during a struggle. The missing charm?

"Thanks for the game, Hollywood." I tossed his keys and left the court. I continued to hold my head high, even as I tripped over a curb for the lighting fixtures. Who put a curb on a tennis court anyway? I pulled over under a tree and checked my phone.

"There you are!" Lois yelled. "I looked everywhere. I thought you stumbled upon the killer and got yourself kidnapped."

"You're partially right."

"What?"

"I did run into the killer. Do you recall the broken keychain at the crime scene? I located a shard of the missing piece on Justin's keys."

"Interesting, but I win this round." Lois crossed her arms and beamed. "Wait until you learn what I found. Not looking promising for the ex-boyfriend."

9

Snooping Around

I dumped a pile of laundry on the couch. The mountain of clothes contained everything I owned, ending my ability to delay the inevitable.

"Run through the waiter's story again, Lois."

She lounged on the recliner, her legs hanging over the armrest. "Jose overheard a gigantic blowup between Justin and Maria. Hardly their first public quarrel but one of their loudest."

"Most of their disputes stemmed from acting. Maria wanted to be regarded as one of the renowned, dramatic actresses."

"Right. She felt Justin didn't take his role on the show seriously. On numerous occasions, she recommended classes to hone his craft-"

I frowned. "Didn't she understand his part? A wisecracking beat cop bucking for a promotion to a detective?"

"This particular shouting match at the club centered around season two of *Prime Suspect*. Justin's role is transitioning into a second or third star while Maria's arc fizzled. The show is planning a romance angle between Justin and Ashton Ashley."

"Despite 'resolving' the feud, our murder vic didn't appreciate her boyfriend cozying up to the girl replacing her. Even on television."

"Exactly. Maria developed a story for her character to hang around in season two which involved an innocent verdict and a romance of her own."

"Aren't four lead characters a crowd?" I dug through my sock pile, marveling at the orphans without matching buddies. "If Maria successfully finagled her way into the show, the other actors would suffer from diminished screen time. A potential motive."

"Talk about vanity." Lois sucked in a breath. "Most of the fat would be trimmed from Ashton's role first, right?"

"Hard to say. But if you cut out the romance and shifted focus to a trial, the newbie might be stuck on desk duty."

Lois tossed one of my missing socks. "Let's step away from the fictional universe into reality. Whose career gains or loses the most?"

"Maria established herself in the industry. She received glowing reviews for her performance including an Emmy nomination."

"I can understand why she wanted to stay."

"Justin meanwhile, is searching for his breakout role." And lying about an amicable breakup.

"He's carrying the stuntman stigma." Lois adjusted the glasses she only wore at home. "Colleagues don't respect his acting chops yet."

"His girlfriend especially." I shifted my folding project to the stack of workout clothes. "Then there's Ashton. She comes with her own fan club and millions of loyal followers. But aside from guest roles, she hasn't appeared on television since leaving her childhood show."

"She's under immense pressure. If this isn't a hit, she might not receive another chance."

"Despite a successful first season, critics think *Prime Suspect* ran its course. Writers can't be happy about Maria's requests to change the script."

"I think you're getting off track, Beckers."

"Fine. Back to *our* prime suspect. Did this last fight spur the breakup?"

"According to my waiter source, yes." Lois consulted colorful notes. "Now after the split is where things get sticky. He couldn't confirm this, but another staff member overheard Maria blackmailing someone involved in the show. She wanted Justin fired and his character killed off."

"Well, Maria certainly did her share to incite violence. Anyone who knows her could be the killer."

Lois tossed her licorice eyes. "You're dancing around the most likely scenario."

"Which is?"

"You know very well. If Maria carries the pull we think she does, Justin's days on the set were numbered. His ex-girlfriend conspired to steal his one shot at stardom. While together, she berated his abilities. In public. Imagine what she said scorned."

"I agree about a motive. The broken keychain puts him at the scene."

"Don't forget, a man fled right before you discovered the body."

"Someone big. I never said a man."

Lois tilted her head with determination in her eyes. "Semantics. The CSI unit found the men's shoeprint outside the studio. While we don't know Justin's size, twelve is usually reserved for someone tall."

"We still need proof. An overheard conversation about blackmail isn't enough for an arrest." My stomach sank. "Or to clear me from the suspect pool."

"How can we find evidence of blackmail? We don't know who she targeted."

"Well, I'm sure the police searched her residence and her trailer, but perhaps they overlooked something innocuous."

"Such as?"

"The script where Justin's character is brutally murdered in an armed robbery minutes before receiving his gold detective's shield."

"You think she stashed an alternate storyline somewhere?"

"Or some type of paperwork detailing the Maria Sinclair Show."

Lois released a sigh like a discharging balloon. "This murder investigation is going to steal ten years off my life. The stress is slowly eating away at every fiber of my body."

"You said the same thing during our four years and A&M. And yet, here you are. Alive and well."

"I'm sure you'll disagree but I suggest searching Maria's trailer first. Our presence on set is far less suspicious than if someone catches us inside her house."

"I concur."

"You do?"

"Don't sound so shocked. You made a swell pitch."

"Which shocks me." Lois disappeared into her bedroom and returned with an overflowing hamper. "Care to accompany me to the laundry room?"

"I don't think there are enough quarters in the world to wash all that. Mount Vesuvius is ready to blow."

The next morning, we arrived on set and received our posts for the day. I further annoyed Sherry, leading to my annex in craft services. The only benefit: all day snacking.

At our lunch break, I met up with Lois. "I brought you fries."

"Ooh. My favorite. Thank you." Lois inspected the Togo box. "No ketchup or mayo?"

"Though it pained me, I grabbed you both." I tossed the packets and cringed as she mixed the dips. It probably tasted better than I thought, but I despised mayonnaise except as an ingredient in something like chicken salad.

With the set quiet, Lois and I slipped to the area of portable dressing rooms. The biggest stars required a trailer to themselves while the second string and guest actors shared.

Ashton brought with her a custom-made Barbie pink trailer. Despite the temptation to snoop, we continued to Maria's. Though not flashy, yellow police tape added an intriguing flare.

I popped my utility knife and cut through the seal.

Lois' eyes widened. "Since when do you carry a switchblade?"

"Relax, Pony Boy. I use this tool to open locks." I examined the simple combination padlock. "Thirty seconds. Time me."

"Where did you possibly learn to pick a lock?"

"I ran with some interesting friends in Lake Falls."

"One day I want to visit your quirky hometown. Half of these people you describe sound fake."

"They are very real." I jiggled the doorknob. "But a story for another time."

The neatness inside Maria's trailer astounded me. Based on cop shows, I expected a mess. Or maybe the disarray was reserved for druggie rock stars. The state of the dressing room made snooping difficult. One pillow out of place would reveal our presence.

"Where should we start?" Lois snapped on crime scene gloves and booties.

"After you, Catherine Willows."

"I refuse to make the same mistake as you. Who plants evidence implicating themselves?"

I cocked my hip, contemplating a defense. "Got any more?"

After gloving-up I opened desk drawers. Fan mail. Receipts. Online ordering. Blank papers. A season one script. Nothing instrumental to our investigation.

I stomped on the wooden floorboards in search of a loose plank. "Nothing."

"How's your safe cracking?"

My neck straightened. "You found a safe?"

"No. I chose now to ask a random question in case we wanted to pull a heist later this evening."

I curtseyed at the sarcastic response. "I left my stethoscope at home. How many combinations could there be, right?" After 1-2-3-4 and Googling her birthday, I tapped my knowledge of safe cracking. "There has to be something here."

Lois opened the kitchen cabinets. "Everything is in its place. Nothing out of the ordinary."

I tiptoed. Something on top of the fridge fluttered. A dining room chair scraped across the floor as I dragged my stool closer. "Eureka."

"What did you find?"

"An envelope."

A barking dog halted my excitement. "Sounds like my Jack Russell Terrier."

"Yours?"

I scooted the curtains as Cutie Pie raced from the trailer. I ducked as footsteps approached. "Someone's coming."

"Not in here, right?" Lois crashed to the floor.

The rattling of keys drew near. "I'm afraid so."

"What are we going to do? If someone finds us here, we're toast."

"And we'll lose the evidence." I stuffed the folder in the back of my jeans and pointed. "When one door closes..."

"God opens a window." Lois crab-walked to the dining room table and cracked the hinged pane. The table partially blocked the exit. With remarkable grace, she squeezed through.

I propped one foot on the cushioned chair and propelled myself over the table. My head smacked the sill and I spilled to the pavement below. Lois caught me by the arm, preventing a complete face plant into the cement.

We pressed against the trailer as Justin Woods slipped underneath the police tape and inside. "What's he doing?"

I shrugged. "Something incriminating." On my toes, I stared through the window.

Justin made a beeline for the hidden safe and entered a five-digit combination. He tucked something under his jacket and fled the scene of his crime.

"Now I really wish I brought my stethoscope."

Lois adjusted her crouch. "What should we do now? Confront him?"

To avoid a hand in the cookie jar moment, I motioned her in the direction of the studio. "With what evidence?"

"He broke into her trailer. Which is marked off by the police."

"So did we." I stroked my chin. "We need to build a case."

"Fine. How about starting with the envelope you found?"

I ripped the seal and unfolded a letter. "This is addressed to Maria's attorney."

"Juicy. What's it say?"

"She's exploring cutting off her brother, Barnett Sinclair. Money is a legitimate motive."

Lois snatched the paper and scanned. "I wonder what size shoes little brother wears."

"We should interview Barnett. Besides being a suspect, he could shed light on his sister's relationship with Justin."

"Do you know where to find him?"

"Next of kin is listed on the crime scene report you photocopied."

"Really?" Lois straightened. "You're welcome."

We navigated L.A. traffic and arrived at the Beverly Hills residence shared by the Sinclair siblings. Constructed in the 1950s, the estate passed through generations of an influential family.

Maria and Barnett's parents added to their wealth by building a prominent talent agency. According to the letter addressed to Maria's attorney, she controlled their inheritance.

"What are we planning?" Lois rubbed her hands together. "Costumes? Disguise? Sneaking in through an underground cellar?"

"I thought we might knock on the front door. Maybe ring the bell if I'm feeling cheeky."

"How is this supposed to work?"

"We play detective. If Barnett isn't the killer, he'll want to answer our questions and help the investigation."

Lois cleared her throat. "What if he is?"

"Stop acting like a chicken. You don't think Barnett's our guy. You accused Justin in the precinct with a lead pipe. No take-backs now."

"I'm afraid because I'm a terrible liar."

"What are we lying about? We *are* investigating Maria's murder."

Lois gulped. "True. Okay, I'm ready."

We climbed a series of stone steps leading to the oversized wooden door. Gargoyles framed the entry, watching our every move. I pounded my fist, channeling a no-nonsense cop.

"Yeah?" The door opened to a long-haired man in flip-flops.

"Mr. Barnett Sinclair?"

He tied his hair into a bun. "Are you paparazzi?"

I held out my empty hands. "You caught us. Our cameraman is hiding in the gargoyles."

A slight smile crept through his trimmed beard. "Fair point. Who are you if not paps?"

"We're private investigators, looking into your sister's murder."

"PIs? Who hired you?"

"I'm not at liberty to divulge my employer, sir." I curled a wispy piece of hair behind my ear. "Would you be so kind to answer a few questions?"

Barnett shifted his weight and stuffed his hands in the pocket of his board shorts. "Anything if it helps find my sister's killer."

Lois opened a notepad as we entered a lavish living room. "Wow. What a place."

"Not my style. But it's a roof over my head." Barnett plopped on a Victorian loveseat.

I perched on the edge of the opposite couch. "Did Maria face problems with anyone? Friends? Someone at work?"

"Everyone loved Maria. She was a light to all who knew her."

Lois coughed. "We heard differently."

"From who, her ex?"

I consulted my notes. "Are you referring to Justin Woods?"

"Yeah. The bum riding her coattails to the top." Barnett leaned forward on his knees. "Sullying her names makes him feel better about being dumped."

"Maria dumped him?" Lois asked.

"Of course. I warned her the guy is bad news but she attracted the worst scum."

"You and Justin butt heads a lot?"

"All the time," Barnett said. "Nervy of him to say I'm mooching off my sister. Our parents put the trust fund in her name because she's the responsible one. Semantics don't make the money any less mine."

Lois twisted her head from me to the brother. "Must have made you angry."

"Yeah. Anytime he dropped by, I hit the gym or went to a club. Anything to not be in the same room. I was thrilled when Maria came to her senses."

I flashed a smile. "Barnett Sinclair. I just realized where I recognized the name. You're the app developer for the Lolly Poppers game."

"More than a game. A total experience, unlike the candy competitors. I create a virtual world with different games and levels. Trading of collector edition lollypops."

Lois twisted her face. "A competitive business to break into."

"You're telling me." Barnett stroked his beard. "I'm always looking for new investors if you ladies are interested. We got a lucrative product poised to make a bunch of money in the coming months."

"You'd be surprised, but detective-ing doesn't pay like it used to." I bit my lip, contemplating my approach to the next question. "Mr. Sinclair, where were you the morning your sister was killed? Between four and seven."

He shot from his seat. "Wait. Am I a suspect?"

"Not at this time," I said. "We are covering our bases with basic questions to everyone who knew Maria."

"By asking about my alibi?"

Lois cleared her throat. "We want to establish a timeline of the events leading to her death."

"Fine. I'm not hiding anything. I was home alone though."

"No one can corroborate?" I asked.

Barnett raked a hand over his dusty brown hair. "The security cameras will show I never left."

"What about Maria?" Lois clicked her pen. "Why wasn't she home?"

"Early set call, I guess. She always keeps weird hours." Barnett swallowed. "I can't believe she's gone."

I sat beside the brother and placed a hand on his shoulder. "Did she mention having problems with anyone or being afraid of something?"

"Maria didn't burden me with her issues. I'm the little brother who's always messing up."

"I've got two of those," Lois snorted.

I caught a spark in Barnett's eye. "What did you remember?"

"Justin. He snooped outside our house the night before Maria... I spotted him lurking in the backyard. I threatened to call the cops, but Maria insisted on handling him. They talked for a bit and he left. She went to work a few hours later."

"Did they argue?" Lois asked.

Barnett twisted his lips. "I can't say. No yelling or anything but they didn't act like old pals."

"Thank you for your time, Mr. Sinclair. If you think of anything else, please give us a call." I ripped a piece of paper from my notebook and scribbled my number.

He folded the scrap and stuffed it in his pocket. "Sure will. I hope you catch the guy."

"Before we leave, do you think we could peruse Maria's room?"

He scratched his head. "The cops took her computer and some other stuff. Not sure if you'll find anything of value."

"Sometimes they don't know where to search."

"Or what to look for," Lois added.

"Upstairs at the end of the hall."

We found Maria's bedroom in a similar state to her trailer. Spotless.

"What are we looking for?" Lois asked.

"I'm not sure. Clues."

"Helpful."

After a sweep of the usual and obvious hiding places – under the mattress, air conditioning duct, floorboards, top drawer – we waved the white flag.

On our way down the hall, I cracked the door to Barnett's room. The polar opposite. Laundry and trash littered the floor. Packing peanuts spilled from a sixty-five-inch Samsung TV box. Who splurged on a television immediately following their sister's death?

"Excuse me?"

I lurched at the brother's voice. "Sorry. A person can get lost in this labyrinth."

He narrowed wispy eyebrows. "You guys should go. I'm leaving for a meeting with my investors."

"Good news?" Lois asked.

He crossed his fingers. "Hope so. I could use a change of luck."

10

Stay Gold Winston

My knee jittered up and down as I waited for my assignment from Sherry. I needed something easy in order to continue the investigation. Barnett Sinclair pointed a strong finger at Justin but I made note of the brother's motive.

I closed my eyes and focused on the movie star. He visited Maria the night before her death. What reason did he have to speak with his ex? Likely something incriminating.

"Is the hour too early for you or are you making a conscious effort to ignore the tone of my voice?"

I gulped as Sherry hovered above me. The dragon lady breathed fire. "I apologize. My mind is somewhere else."

"Ah. Well, should we pause the meeting while you catch up or may I continue?"

"It won't happen again."

Sherry sucked in a breath and adjusted the glasses perched on her nose. "As I started to say before the unnecessary interruption, a small faction of the cast will be on set this afternoon. Filming will only last a couple of hours as they return to a normalized routine. This means everything must be in tip-top shape."

Sherry's assistant passed out assignments. Lois unfolded her envelope and cringed. "Hair and makeup? I don't even wear makeup."

"And you rarely brush your hair."

"The only perk to my straight, sleek locks – no tangles."

I ripped open my post and grinned. "You're looking at Winston's newest friend."

"Who's Winston?"

"The golden retriever on the series. His character works in the K9 Unit as a drug-sniffing dog."

"I'm glad I'm not assigned there." Lois held her breath. "Dogs scare me."

"Winston is a well-trained show dog. Far from a rabid killer."

My phone buzzed across the table. I punched the decline button, ducking another call from Agent Cornwallis. Before he made further accusations, I hoped to discover evidence on a real suspect.

Sherry dismissed the meeting and I skipped to meet the trainer. By far my best assignment since becoming a gopher. He gave specific instructions for Winston's care. Where I was allowed to walk him. What he ate and when. And other rules to prevent him from acting like a dog.

We exited Winston's personal trailer and I clipped the leash to his collar. Rubbing behind his ears, I resisted the urge to baby talk. "Hey, Winnie. I'm sure your trainer means well, but I'm way more relaxed. Today, you can act like a puppy... if you want. No pressure." He tilted his head and soulful brown eyes stared at me. "Want to go for a walk?"

He barked.

I expanded the designated walking path and the show dog to choose our route. Winston enjoyed investigating new scents and chasing leaves. When we reached the old west set, he charged after a plastic jackrabbit, the disappointment evident when he caught up. "Movie magic, Winnie."

His nose sniffed the air, prompting an idea.

"Any chance you're a method actor? A bomb-sniffing dog could theoretically find other smells, right?" I twisted my head. "Maybe this is crazy, but if you catch Maria's scent you might follow it and lead me to evidence?"

Winston rubbed his face with a paw as if shielding his eyes from my nutty idea.

"You're right. I'm a wackadoodle."

He lifted his head and wagged his tail. "What is it, boy?"

My Jack Russell Terrier darted from the shadowed set, approaching with hesitance. "Cutie Pie, you're back! This handsome fella is Winston. I call him Winnie because it sounds less pretentious. Care to introduce yourself?"

Cutie Pie took a hesitant step forward and Winston got overeager. "Sit. Lie down."

The show dog did as directed. With the bigger animal submissive, Cutie Pie approached, touching nose to nose. Both dogs wagged their tails at warp speed.

I rubbed behind Cutie Pie's ears and she licked my hand. "What's so homey about the old west saloon?" I carried the puppy underneath my arm so she wouldn't escape and entered the set.

I flipped on a light and scanned the area. Nothing out of place or cozy for a homeless pup. I sat Cutie Pie down to roam free. She darted under the bar and dug into a pile of cloth, making herself comfortable. I gasped as the realization hit me.

Cutie Pie made her bed on a bloody t-shirt. A Louisville Slugger, smeared in blood, propped against the wall.

"Don't tell me you're the killer?" I sighed. "Welp. I guess I should return the many phone calls of Cornwallis."

As we waited for the CBI agent to arrive, the dogs played in the abandoned street. They kicked up dust as they ran after each other and fetched sticks. Winston grinned from ear to ear, enchanted by his new friend. The timid nature of Cutie Pie dissipated as she began to trust us.

"What is the meaning of this?" Sherry's voice yet again startled. "What's he doing here?"

"You assigned me to dog walking."

"I am aware. Why is he canoodling with the mutt?"

"She's not a mutt. And they're playing. Being dogs."

"Winston is a purebred show animal. He makes more money per hour than you can dream of." She challenged me with a hand on her hip. "He is filming a scene in two hours and he's covered in dust. Can you guess who will be blamed for this?"

"You can't keep him cooped up and clean all the time. He needs to be a dog."

"He's a performer."

"Right. And he loves the attention. But what does an hour of fun hurt?"

Sherry pinched her fingers. "You are this close to wearing through my patience. Bring him back to his trailer, now."

"I can't."

Steam billowed. "And why not?"

"I'm waiting for the CBI."

"Why?"

"I found the murder weapon."

"Murder weapon?" Sherry's posture bolted upright. "In the saloon?"

"Yeah. A baseball bat covered in blood. Cornwallis told me to hold tight until security came. He should be by shortly for my statement."

"How did you stumble upon the murder weapon?"

"Only a theory, but I think Cutie Pie witnessed the killing. She's been sleeping on the evidence the last few days."

"The mutt found the murder weapon. Just perfect."

My forehead creased. "Isn't this a good thing?"

"The circus will shut down filming again while they investigate. Makes no difference the crime scene is on the other side of the studio. They'll interrogate each one of us ad nauseam."

"The price of catching a killer, I guess."

"Whatever. Collect Winston and I'll return him to his trailer."

Cutie Pie growled as Cruella hauled away her new friend. "It's okay. We'll play with him again."

Agent Cornwallis darted into view and slid to a stop on his worn loafers. Mustard stained his necktie flapping in the breeze. "Crime scene unit is on their way. Where's the evidence?"

"Inside."

Cornwallis removed a napkin from his pocket and nudged the bat. "Cov... Covered in blood. How did you come across the murder weapon?"

I again explained my dumb luck with dubious results.

"Uh-huh." He scribbled in a notebook. "You happened to find the body and then the baseball bat some days later. You're a real fortunate type person, Miss Roberson."

I ignored the mistaken identity. "Not hardly."

"We gonna find any... any of your prints on the baseball bat?" he stuttered.

"Not unless someone planted them."

His forehead crinkled. "Are you hinting at a departmental conspiracy?"

"Why don't you ever work with a partner, Agent Cornwallis?"

"I do. But Gerrity only works for his pension these days. He ain't known for hitting the streets. More likely hitting the buffet line if you know what I mean."

Odd. Cornwallis was the competent cop of the bunch. CBI could really use a consultant to save their bacon. "Any leads on the killer?"

"Not of your concern."

"I thought your many calls might be to update me on the investigation."

"I want... I wanted to plug some inconsistencies in your story." The crime scene unit busted into the saloon with their kits and UV lights. The chaos disrupted the agent's line of inquiry. "We'll discuss your secrets later. You can go."

My mind raced through possibilities as Cutie Pie and I returned to the set. A baseball bat as a murder weapon told a story – a crime of passion and opportunity. The killer grabbed something handy.

11

Lorelai

Lois plopped on the couch and released a dramatic lion moan. "I'm dead."

"What happened to you?"

She swiped at the cosmetics caked on her face. "Don't ask. The hair and makeup girls got bored with filming postponed."

"So, they decided to play a mean joke on you?"

"Too much?"

I squinted and closed one eye. "Well, they say the camera requires a thicker base. Are you auditioning for the Joker?"

"Since you found the murder weapon, our investigation is finished, right?"

"Unless they find my fingerprints." I tilted my head. "Or no prints."

Lois blew hair from her face. "Being a detective is exhausting. I'm ready to unwind."

I leaned for the remote and selected *Gilmore Girls* on Netflix. "This is the one where Lorelai drinks coffee and teases Luke."

"Didn't we see this one?"

The theme song blasted through the speakers 'Where You Lead, I Will Follow'. Cutie Pie chose the same moment to come out of hiding. "You must be a Gilmore fan."

Lois yanked her feet to the couch. "What's that?"

"A Canis lupus familiaris."

"Why is it here?"

"I rescued her."

"Becky, I'm afraid of dogs."

"No, you aren't. You never met the right one. Lois, meet Lorelai Gilmore."

"You're naming her after the show?" Lois shook her head. "We can't keep her."

Lorelai and I flashed matching puppy dog faces. "But she's a cutie pie. Homeless and alone."

"You're a terrible roommate." She released a breath. "Fine. We can keep her but don't let her jump on me."

Lorelai hopped on the couch and curled in my lap. "She's already making herself at home."

Lois tapped the pause button. "Do you think the bat belongs to Justin?"

"He plays baseball and supposedly keeps equipment in his trailer. It is a souvenir from an early project, signed by the cast. The blood constricted my view of the Louisville Slugger, but it looked autographed."

"Welp, one case solved. Can *Prime Suspect* survive losing another star?"

"Who knows?"

"Gosh, we could be out of jobs soon."

My mind drifted and a queasiness formed in my stomach. I couldn't shake the gnawing sense of dread. As if I left something incomplete. If the killer possessed the fortitude to remove the weapon from the crime scene, why did he stash it at the studio? Besides, anyone working on a cop show would remember to wipe away fingerprints. The baseball bat wasn't a smoking gun.

"Beckers wake up." Lois burst through my bedroom door.

Lorelai barked at the intrusion as I squinted at my clock. "Why are you waking me at 5:30?"

She flashed a headline. "Justin Woods killed ex-girlfriend in a jealous rage. Rumor is the police tied him to the scene and his arrest is imminent."

I shook the fog invading my brain. "Where are you getting your information?"

"The news is all over Twitter. A blogger named Phyllis Montoya broke the story and it is going viral."

"And we know how reliable Twitter is."

"This means you're officially in the clear. No more murder suspicion." Lois closed the door but I never returned to my peaceful slumber. I agonized over my case notes, searching for the missing piece.

A few hours later, we arrived on set to an eerie calm. As if the news failed to reach the studio. I wandered the grounds, avoiding my assignment as my mind continued to churn.

At craft services, a commotion drew my attention. I ducked inside as a plate flew across the room and shattered into the wall.

"This isn't supposed to happen," the voice squealed. "*Prime Suspect* is my second chance. I refuse to repeat more of the same dribble. The shadow of my childhood fame is hovering like a..."

"Rain cloud?"

"Yeah sure." Ashton Ashley placed hands on her narrow waist. "Maria tried her best to ruin my life from the moment the show hired me. She saw the flashing neon signs. Easily replaced by a younger, blonder, beauty." She twisted a lock of hair. "Now my world continues to crumble because of incompetent writers like you, Norv. These new pages are complete and utter garbage. My character would never say these things."

"Those are the Miranda Rights, read to a suspect under arrest."

"Well, I don't think they fit the scene. Jill is a competent, cunning female cop. She shouldn't be chasing suspects. Who would run from me?"

"Well without ah... the chase sequence, act three is dry."

"Not my problem, Norv. I thought you consider yourself an intellectual. A witty writer with snappy one-liners. Yet my character reads like a prescription drug commercial. Justin on the other hand gets all the laughs. Joke. Joke. Joke. Joke." She flipped a page in the script. "Joke. Who's he... I can't think of a comedian."

"Jerry Seinfeld?"

"Who? Whatever. Doesn't matter. My fans, millions of followers, will tune into your little program and make it a rating success. They expect a certain level of entertainment. Smart and hilarious like my social media platform. By hiring me, the show agreed to represent my brand image. The Ashton Ashley brand doesn't accept bottom feeder, cesspool dribble."

"So, I guess you're telling me you didn't like the script?"

She patted Norv's cheek. "Channel some of your cheeky biz into the writing instead."

I leaned around the corner for a better view and smacked into the buffet table. Paper cups and plastic stir sticks spilled across the floor.

"Oh my goodness, are you okay?" Ashton dashed over and cupped my elbow. "You really wiped out."

I gulped, dreading her wrath when she discovered my eavesdropping. "I'm a klutz."

"For a tiny little thing you sure made a whopper of a mess." Ashton scooped my spilled supplies. "Don't be embarrassed. I'm the biggest goof of all. With long luscious legs like mine, you might think I possessed the grace of a ballerina. No such luck with my two left feet."

My brow crinkled at the 180-degree spin. Perhaps Double-A was a better actress than I realized. Two could play her game. "You don't know how relieved I am to hear so. I'm a nervous wreck around movie stars. I see... well stars."

She waved. "Aw. I'm flattered."

"Seeing all y'all in person is a dream. I'm a huge fan of the show and I loved your sitcom growing up."

A muscle above her brow pulsed. A practiced smile replaced the discomfort. "I'm blessed to be part of another cast with such a fantastic cultural impact."

"I only wish the fans experienced you and Maria sharing the screen. I rooted for y'all to patch the feud. You seemed so alike with the potential to be great friends in real life."

Ashton coughed. My act chipping away at her armor. "I only wish the resolve came sooner. Our friendship - cut down before it had the chance to fully blossom."

Wow. She was good. "I learned the cops are closing in on the murderer. But it isn't who the press suspects."

"What?" The façade splintered. "Who else are the police after but Justin? He's as guilty as they come."

"Their focus on him is apparently a red herring to draw out the real killer." I made a show of zipping my lips and throwing away the key. "But don't spread this revelation. I'm not supposed to know much less share."

"Sure. Sure." Her blue eyes twitched, mascara clumping. "But the bat, the murder weapon. How can they think it isn't Justin? All the evidence..." she petered out. "No matter. I'm sure they are handling the investigation. What do I know, I only play a cop on television?"

"I'm so looking forward to seeing you on the show. Anything you can tease about your character? We have some of the best writers in the business, I'm sure they help bring your part to life."

She swiped hair from her eyes. "The level of talent is something I did not expect." She shot a passive-aggressive expression over her shoulder. "I am looking forward to representing a strong female cop. A role model for young girls."

"I hope we clear the hurdles and resume shooting. I overheard the producer when I delivered coffee..." I petered out. "Never mind, I don't want to gossip about secondhand information."

"Are they thinking of canceling?"

"Losing Maria is a horrendous blow to ratings. Some fans are talking about boycotting. One more issue and the producers might pull the plug."

"Her army of 500 followers? I think we'll survive." Ashton pursed glossed lips. "I mean this season is a tribute. I think once people realize, they'll be able to enjoy."

"You underestimate the loyalty of fans. True supporters will go to extreme lengths for their idols. I suppose it's hard to imagine unless you're in her shoes?"

"Did you hit your head when you fell? Maria's fan club is minuscule compared to my army. I tweet about a cough and people from around the world send me get-well messages. Pictures accidentally snapped from the inside of my purse go viral, #EpicFail #RealProblems."

Ashton needed a lesson in what constituted real problems. "Wow, sounds like the feud isn't nearly as dead as Maria."

"Who exactly are you?"

"Me? I'm nobody."

"Obviously. But why are you so question-y all of a sudden? I'm usually better at diagnosing reporters."

"I'm simply a humble lunch lady in craft services."

"Smart play getting me riled up. I should learn to watch out for the little, scrappy ones." She patted my head.

"Your whole lion in sheep's clothing façade won't last."

"Oh, dear. It always does. All about branding and spin. Public blowups are #Hangry or #PastMyBedTime. The people are forgiving and love when I behave like a real person with problems."

I sucked in a breath, shifting tactics. Double-A didn't respond as I hoped to someone challenging her and calling out her phoniness. "Maybe I will learn a thing or two from you."

"You want to act?"

"Doesn't everyone who moves to Hollywood?"

Ashton cocked her head. "I'm not searching for a protégé."

"Never hurts to ask." The flattery planted a seed for the next time I might need to talk to Ashton. "Good luck with your scene this afternoon."

As I stomped to the main building, I checked my recent calls list and hovered over Cornwallis' name. I wanted an update on the case but I also knew what his answer would be. Waiting for the lab results gave me an ulcer. I couldn't wait to be free and clear of suspicion.

I cut through a cardboard cutout town and approached the trailer area. A strong hand gripped my wrist, spinning my momentum. I opened my mouth to scream when a hand muffled the plea.

Justin. Would I become his next victim?

12

Guilty Until Proven Innocent

I chomped on the attacker's hand and swiped my leg at his kneecap. He buckled to the floor and I swung my bag at his head. He caught the oversized purse and wrestled away the weapon.

Justin Woods wobbled, shaking his wounded hand. "You bit me."

"Because you tried to make me your next victim."

"You're pretty scrappy."

"So I've been told."

"You a stunt double in your spare time?"

I chewed the corner of my lip. "I'll give you five seconds to leave before I scream bloody murder."

"I guess you formed your own conclusion about my guilt."

"If the shoe fits. What size do you wear, by the way?"

His brows twitched. "Thirteen."

A notch bigger than the print outside the crime scene. "Why are you attacking me? I'm getting too close to the truth?"

"I wish." He scrubbed blonde stubble on his chin. "I didn't kill my ex-girlfriend. The police are following a dummy trail and refuse to listen to reason. As soon as their forensics reports come back, I'll be arrested."

"Why are you coming to me?"

"You found the body. You asked questions at the club. You discovered the murder weapon. Doesn't take a real detective to follow those clues. You're investigating."

"So what? I tend to agree with the cops."

"No, you don't." Justin edged closer. "In your gut, you don't believe I'm a killer." He tucked a strand of hair behind my ear.

I swatted his hand. "Innocent people don't default to charming manipulation."

"Hey, at least you think I'm charming."

"You switch between emotions so quickly, are you schizophrenic?" My hands flailed as I spoke, showing the Italian on my mother's side.

"Frantic. I'm hours away from an arrest warrant. I'm desperate for someone to believe me. Can you give me five minutes? If you don't trust me after my time expires, I'll drop it."

"Why me? I'm sure you can afford a professional PI."

"I hired one a few days ago. He's learned squat." He paced to his trailer and opened the door.

"No way I voluntarily entering the abode of a murder suspect."

"There are ears everywhere."

"Paranoid much? Are you claiming abduction by aliens too?"

"Yes. But a story for another time." He motioned to the door. "Please?"

I entered but stood by the exit, ten feet from the accused. "If you tell one lie, I end this little interview."

"Fine."

"Tell me about your PI. Why did you hire him?"

"The day Maria turned up dead and the CBI questioned me, I realized I was in trouble. The jilted ex is always the number one suspect. I couldn't take the chance so I hired a guy I trusted. He consulted on the show last year."

"I don't remember a storyline involving a private detective."

"Nah, Giuseppe provided expertise on the mob arc. He's not connected or anything. He did a research paper on the *Myth of the Mob* at USC. He's a hefty Italian looking dude, always gets the Corleone comparison."

"Is his office near the boardwalk?"

"Above a restaurant."

My mind flashed to when we followed Justin to the beach. "Did you stop by and give him a wad of cash before tennis at the club?"

"You were stalking me."

"Guilty... no wait, that's you." I opened my notepad. "So, you didn't pay Giuseppe to eliminate your girlfriend."

"Of course not."

"Do you have an alibi for the murder? Between four and seven a.m.?"

"I woke up at five and went for a run on the beach."

"Cliché."

"Excellent cardio."

"Can anyone corroborate?" I asked. The question made me feel like a real cop.

"I ran alone."

I pointed to the Fitbit strapped to his wrist. "Do you obsessively log your exercise?"

"I keep track."

"Give me your phone." I opened the app and checked his activity. Asleep until a few minutes after five followed by an hour and a half run. "Geez. Are you nuts?" Though not ironclad, the fitness tracker provided doubt.

"I do wind sprints when I'm stressed. I was a tad out of sorts that morning."

"Did the stress stem from the argument between you and Maria the night before her death?"

"How?"

"Barnett Sinclair spilled the beans."

"Rat." Justin stroked a hand through his hair. "M.J. and I didn't spilt as amicably as I previously claimed. The show's not big enough for the two of us and all that jazz."

"You argued about the show?"

"She was determined to pressure the producers into firing me. She would sell her soul to the devil if it meant the end of my tenure."

"Do you comprehend how this motive thing works?"

His chin dimpled. "You said no lies. If the truth makes me appear guilty, so be it."

"Tell me about the baseball bat I found. It is yours, right?"

"Unfortunately. And I'm sure my fingerprints are all over it."

"You kept the Louisville Slugger inside your trailer?" I asked.

"Hanging on the wall."

"The day we met when you were incognito as a Dodger, I bumped into you at the old west set. Same place as the murder weapon. Strange coincidence."

"Every time I'm at the studio, I go by the ghost town. John Wayne is my hero and I'm a sucker for westerns. I go to the livery and I imagine my next break in a new wave of western flicks. I practice the quick draw like I'm a kid in the backyard again. But people don't care about those movies anymore. It's all superheroes, explosions, SFX, and damaged anti-heroes. A silly dream."

"Your visits to the set, are others aware?"

"I'm not embarrassed by it. I playact for a living."

"Meaning if someone wanted to set you up, they'd come to your unlocked trailer, steal an autographed baseball bat, kill your ex, and plant the murder weapon at your favorite haunt."

"Crafty."

I sighed. "Unlikely."

"This is a classic frame job." He swung his arms outward. "I work on a cop show. The murder is too sloppy. First, I wouldn't assault someone using a weapon with direct ties to me. Second, I wipe off my prints. Third, I destroy the evidence."

"Excellent, you're making notes for your next killing spree."

"Come on, you're aware of how these procedurals go. The one thing they teach you is how to clean a crime scene."

"If you didn't kill her, who did?"

"Beats me. M.J. lived for ruffling feathers. When she didn't get her way, lookout."

"If you expect me to believe your story, I need alternative suspects. Plausible leads."

"I don't like the idea of accusing people I work with of murder."

"Fine. Enjoy spending your golden years in the hoosegow."

"Barnett pointed a finger at me but his nose is plenty dirty. His app is a colossal flop. He's been hitting up investors coast to coast but no one is taking the bait. Maria prepared to cut him off and kick him out."

"He inherits the entirety of their trust funds?"

"Giving him motive."

I tucked a flyaway behind my ear. "Interesting theory, but he alibied out. Anyone else?"

"This is a pure gut reaction with no proof but Ashton Ashley gives me a vibe. She switches between personalities with the flip of a button."

"I noticed."

Justin narrowed his eyes. "I thought she fooled you with the inspiring speech."

"I fibbed to wind you up." I tapped my chin. "If I believed you, and I'm not saying I do, why would Ashton frame you?"

"I'm the easy patsy. Motive, means, opportunity. She's smarter than people realize."

"But she needs this show to happen. Losing two leads is risky."

"But perhaps a worthy gamble. Her name climbs the ranks with me and her nemesis gone."

"I don't picture Ashton taking a bat to someone's head. Even her enemy."

Justin shoved hands in his pocket. "I learned early on not to underestimate her. Beyond the outer candy is a rotten center."

"Did you pull the metaphor from some cheesy dialogue?"

"No?" He laughed. "Maybe. I don't think any of my words are my own anymore."

I sighed. "What do you think I can do?"

"I can tell you buy my story, if only partially. I need someone to help me find the truth. Who better to hire than the snoopy gal who found the body? At least we know you didn't kill her."

"About that..."

His green eyes widened. "You didn't, did you?"

"Of course not. But my name might be right below yours on the suspect list."

"How?"

"I dropped my ID badge which somehow wedged under the body. The specifics are hazy but the CBI isn't too bright."

"Well, I guess we both found a reason to pursue the investigation."

The trailer door swung open. "You're a tough one to find." Agent Cornwallis dangled handcuffs from his finger. "Am I gonna need these?"

13

Downtown

My heart hammered as I focused on the handcuffs swinging in Cornwallis' grasp. I pointed a finger at my chest. "Are you talking to me or him?"

"Huh? Roberson, why do you keep showing up everywhere?" The CBI agent blinked. "You, actor boy, put on the bracelets."

"Am I being arrested?" Justin asked.

"Looks like we're heading in the general direction." Cornwallis combed through his thin russet hair. "Unless you can offer a reasonable explanation at the station."

"You're after the wrong guy," Justin said.

I touched his arm. "Your story reads like every criminal claiming innocence."

"I thought you believed me?"

I made a face for the agent's benefit and lowered my voice. "Lawyer-up."

"I'll look guilty."

"Newsflash, Hollywood."

Justin extended his wrists. "Alright, Corny. Make sure to call my lawyer when we arrive at HQ."

"You want to play this card? Fine. But once we allow attorneys in the room, muddling things up, I can't help you."

I bounced on my tiptoes. "You're hauling in one of New York's finest, not a two-bit dealer. He is aware of his rights."

"Whose side are you on, Roberson?"

"R-O-B-I-N-S-O-N. I'm on the side of the truth."

"Now who's speaking in cheesy movie lines?" Justin ducked as he exited. "Agent Cornwallis, I'm willing to answer your questions because I am innocent. But my lawyer will be present in case you already decided on my guilt."

The agent pointed a stubby finger at me. "Don't forget, you and I still need to talk."

"Looking forward to it, Chief."

Lois charged into the props department and bent at the waist. She wheezed, winded from the sprint. "Did you hear?"

"About?"

"The arrest. Everyone is chattering about Woods being hauled away in handcuffs."

"Justin is innocent."

Lois' entire body slouched, conveying her irritation. "Not this again. Your silly celebrity crush is melting your brain."

"No. Before the crack CBI team arrived, I interviewed Justin. He plugged all the holes in his story and provided a solid alibi. I believe him."

"What alibi?"

"Out for jog."

"Oh my. Talk about ironclad."

"His Fitbit confirms the route. I didn't come to this lightly." I led Lois to a park bench and relayed my conversation with the actor.

"What about the secret file he snatched from Maria's safe? Did you forget about his snooping in her trailer?"

"It didn't come up." My mouth twisted. "I'll ask him next time I run into him."

"Behind bars?"

"He hired us to find the real killer."

"A wannabe actress and a struggling director? Sure, who wouldn't hire us?" Lois combed bangs from her face. "With the show likely ending we can use the extra rent money. How much is he paying?"

"We didn't exactly discuss price."

"Well, he isn't in a position to negotiate. I'll draw up a contract." Lois jotted a note with a neon gel pen.

"You realize, Lo Vo, if you cut out your pen expense, we can save enough for three months' rent."

The nickname elicited an eye roll. "These are fancy pens. They write super thin and pretty."

"And cost more than my entire outfit put together."

"Anyway, if not Justin, who?"

"He mentioned the brother."

"He provided an equally hackable alibi."

"But I'm getting a stronger vibe from Ashton Ashley."

Lois nodded. "This we can agree on."

For the next few minutes, we discussed the actresses' blowup and her multiple personality disorder. "Interviewing her is tricky. I worry mention of the murder will spark our demise."

"Did you develop any rapport with her?"

I swished my hand in a 'so-so' signal. "Flattery is our best shot."

Lois swiped her phone and read a text message. "Sherry called an emergency, all-personnel meeting. Hopefully, we can interview Ashton afterward."

We hustled across the studio and entered a packed conference room. Sherry banged a thermos on the table. "Settle down. This isn't gossip hour." She donned her reading glasses. "I just came from a conference with the producers and our showrunner. Losing Justin is a huge blow to both our morale and the show itself. However, we decided to push onward with season two."

"I'm shocked," Lois whispered. "How?"

"To cancel now is ridiculous," I said. "Free press alone will skyrocket ratings."

"No one can predict what Justin's future holds and we don't want to speculate." Sherry read from her script and the words lacked her normal conviction. "Therefore, we are proceeding without his character. The writers are working on an alternative B story to fill the void."

Ashton Ashley raised her hand. "This may be unorthodox, but did you consider recasting his part?"

"We are exploring numerous avenues. In the meantime, filming will continue with our other actors." Sherry clapped. "Business as usual, people. I don't want to discover otherwise from your superiors." She dismissed the meeting and the gossip resumed.

I elbowed through the crowd and trailed Ashton outside. Lois tugged on my sleeve. "Are we sure about this?"

"No." I cupped my hands around my mouth. "Ashton! I'm so glad we caught up with you."

She squinted, attempting to place the recognition. "Hello."

"We met this morning at craft services."

"Oh, the clumsy girl."

Lois snickered. "Quite the name you're making for yourself."

I ignored the snide remark. "How are you holding up, Ashton? This must be incredibly difficult, losing two co-stars."

Her hand covered her heart. "I'm honestly in shock. Literally shaking. But I can't worry about outside forces. This season is a tribute to our fans."

"Too many bad omens." Lois waved her arms. "This place carries a troublesome aura. Cloudy mojo."

I frowned at her insincere superstitious Asian role. She came off sounding only a little *stitious*.

"I sensed the same about this place. Can you conjure any ancient Chinese remedies to put us back on track?" Ashton arched a perfectly shaped brow. "How stupid do you think I am? What are you two after?"

"We decided to play Nancy Drew." I leaned closer and lowered my voice. "Turns out Justin provided an alibi for the murder."

"Says who?" Ashton scoffed. "The police arrested him."

"All for show so they can draw out the real killer," Lois said.

"And you two are what, going to find him first?"

"Or her," I added. "I managed to sneak a peek at the suspect list Agent Cornwallis is compiling. Surprised me to catch your name at the top."

"My name? What possible reason would I have to kill Maria?"

I lifted my shoulders. "His note said, 'no account for the murder window' which means you had opportunity."

"I gave the little troll my alibi. He is probably too busy drooling over meeting a star to remember. I attended a yoga class with fifty other women. I live-Tweet my routine every other morning and I checked in on Instagram. Millions of people can confirm I didn't bludgeon Maria."

"What a relief." I swiped a hand across my forehead. "I don't think the show would survive losing you."

Lois braided a small section of her hair. "A few names on the suspect list surprised us."

"What do you know about the Chalet on the Hills Country Club?" I asked.

"Is someone associated with the club under suspicion?"

My eyes drifted as I pretended to recall. "I can't remember the name but a lady witnessed Maria arguing with an influential member."

"This is typical. The same day I'm confirmed, Maria manages to block me from the grave." Ashton cocked her hip. "My aunt fought for months for my confirmation but Maria swayed the board time and time again. She kept logs of blackmail on everyone. But Vera Killgallen doesn't scare so easily."

Lois' eyes widened. "Maria conspired to keep you out of the club?"

"Astonishing, right? As if my presence would taint the water. I think she grew jealous of losing her position in the community."

"Your aunt often disagreed with Maria?" I asked.

"Yeah. But the police are crazy if they think Vera is capable of murder. Sure, Maria caused a nuisance for us, but it was only a matter of time. With my influential fans and connections to the media, the club couldn't find a legitimate cause to deny my application. And Vera is up for president. When she wins, she will overthrow Maria's cronies on the board."

"Unless Maria decided to run."

Ashton's face paled. "No matter. I'm in now and after my confirmation tomorrow evening, there's nothing anyone can do."

"Thank you for your time, Ashton."

Her eyes narrowed. "Watch your backs. Your little investigation could get messy."

Lois shivered. "Did she threaten us?"

"Who can tell?" I waved. "Vera Killgallen is now near the top of our suspect list."

"Ugh. Are you going to suggest another trip to the club?"

"Not quite yet. I need to visit an old friend first."

14

New Evidence

I yanked the peaked cap lower over my eyes as I snuck downstairs into the coroner's office. The police costume bulked around my short arms as I reached for the door handle. I knocked on the frame. "Dr. Eklund?"

The M.E. spun on his stool and lifted a face shield. "Officer Robinson, right?"

"Splendid memory. How did your wife like the flowers?"

"Smashing success, Officer. I owe you one."

"Is it rude if I cash in right away?"

"Name your price. I'm forever in your debt. I impressed Esmeralda by taking the time to find her birth month flower thing. Probably saved my marriage."

"I'm happy to help." I looped a thumb through my belt, attempting cop posture. "I wanted an update on the Maria Sinclair case. Are the labs back on the murder weapon?"

"Give me a sec." He jerked at the loud Hawaiian shirt collar protruding from his lab coat and slid over to the computer. "A Louisville Slugger is consistent with the victim's head wounds. Trace found slivers of maple in the wound track. Fingerprints are a match to lead suspect Justin Woods."

"His prints are in the system?"

"Uh no. The boys printed him this afternoon, confirming the identity." Eklund adjusted glasses straight out of the 1980s. "We pulled an unidentified smudge on the barrel."

"Any news on the footprint? Or DNA under the vic's fingernails?"

"DNA is still out but we verified the donor is female."

I froze. "The skin cells under Maria's nails are from a woman?"

"Yeah. The defense attorney will enjoy a field day with that one." Eklund smacked the band of his rubber gloves.

"What about the bloody t-shirt?"

"Ah yes. The weird one." He opened a folder. "Blood type matches the victim. Smear pattern suggests the killer used the shirt to wipe blood rather than worn during the murder. The strange thing is we found no skin cells, sweat stains, or trace on the material. Out of the box new."

"Meaning what?"

"All considered, I don't think we collected enough to hold the guy." Eklund shoved a hand through white-blonde hair. "An ID badge under the body places a woman at the scene. Along with the female skin cells, we've got reasonable doubt in spades."

"ID badge?"

"One of those studio passes for an assistant named Rebecca Roberson. CSI technicians determined the body fell on the ID, placing the woman at the murder. We're waiting on a few other tests to secure a warrant for her DNA."

I gulped. "Are you close?"

"Hard to say. The badge alone isn't enough. Agent Cornwallis is working on every angle."

"That he is."

Dr. Eklund stood and tidied the autopsy table. "How long you been on the job, Robinson?"

"Fresh out of the academy. This is extra credit research. I hope to make detective one day."

I hated to lie to the doctor, but my statement technically held true. I recently graduated from college and fancied myself an amateur investigator. The semantics helped ease my guilt.

"You'll turn into a fine detective."

"Thanks, Doc."

I exited the Medical Examiner's office with a thumping heart. Despite the recent developments, Justin and I still topped the suspect list.

"Excuse me officer, is the ME in?"

I froze at the familiar stutter. My eyes landed on scuffed loafers as I ducked my head. "Yup."

"Th... Thanks."

I tipped my cap and listened to the retreating footsteps. Cornwallis rounded the corner out of view. I increased my gait and hustled to the stairs.

"Hey!" Realization dawned as Cornwallis swiveled on his heel.

Channeling dreaded high school drills, I charged the steps. My short legs attacked the task and I hit the ground floor running. After a few cross looks from spectators, I slowed my pace to a brisk walk. I leaned my chin against the prop radio, pretending to engage in an emergency call.

Polished floors caused me to skid into a stop as I darted around a corner. I plowed face-first into a lab tech carrying a stack of reports. We spilled to the floor, sliding like cartoon characters.

"Sorry." I scooped some documents and indicated the radio. "In a rush. Got called on a 108."

"You, Officer? Hold on!" Cornwallis said.

The papers fluttered to the ground as I took off. I scanned signs, attempting to find an escape. In the excitement, I managed to turn myself around. A thumping heart updated my internal clock. Cornwallis gained on me. If he caught me impersonating a policeman, he would arrest me for sure.

I gulped, contemplating my options. The emergency exit at the end of the hall. No, the alarm would sound. I slipped inside the women's bathroom and slammed my back against the door.

"Running from someone?" A uniform cop stood at the sink, washing her hands.

"Fleeing the fuzz." My laugh carried an unnatural hiccup.

A knock vaulted me from the door. "Roberson? I spotted you."

"An old boyfriend?" the female officer asked.

The question sparked a plan. "A bumbling CBI agent. Twice my age but continues to ask me out." I tilted my head. "Would you be willing to help me pull a fast one?"

Cornwallis knocked again. "Roberson?"

The cop curled wispy pieces of hair around her ears. "My pleasure." She waved me to a stall and opened the door. "In case you can't read, this is the lady's room."

"Ah... I..." the agent fumbled for words. "Is anyone inside with you?"

"No."

"I'm sorry, I guess I thought you were someone else."

The door squeaked closed. "You're all set, honey."

I released a breath. "Thank you."

"Any time."

I waited a few minutes before peeking into the hall. After checking to make sure the coast was clear, I returned to my car in the parking lot. In the safety of my apartment, I stashed the uniform under my bed for future use.

Lorelai pushed up against my leg, wielding her new squeaker. I tossed the doughnut in a frisbee motion and she slid across the hardwood in pursuit. She returned with a beaming smile and making a racket. I dangled the toy and she leaped like a bunny, snatching it from the air.

"Hey Becky, take a gander at this." Lois knocked on my ajar door, displaying her iPad.

I scrolled through a Twitter feed. "People are bad-mouthing Maria? Sort of poor form."

"No talent. Witch to work with. Diva. Backstabbing."

"I guess I'm not surprised. Every post on social media represents a polarizing opinion."

"Check out the common denominator with these people."

"What?"

"They are all loyal Ashton Ashley followers."

I examined the Tweets closer. "Read this one from two weeks ago."

Lois pinched the screen. "Maria spent the last five years clinging to younger roles and refusing to admit her age. A minuscule fan club not enough to save her role. Trying to get rid of the queen? #EpicFail."

"Continue to the next one."

"Literally shaking after hearing AA message. #FanTribute #PrimeSavior." Lois peered over the screen. "Obsessed much?"

"Faking."

"What do you mean?"

"These Tweets are straight from the horse's mouth. This *Ashley fan girl 91* is none other than the teeny-bopper herself."

"Wait, she's pretending to be a fan to insult Maria online? Mighty desperate."

"I can't prove my theory, but I listened to Ashton say the same phrases today. Not a coincidence."

Lois blinked, clearing the fog. "What's the implication here?"

"If Maria discovered Ashton's alter ego, the phony account might ruin her. She's all about transparency with fans. Turns out one of her top followers is a fake."

"This girl is one mango short of a fruit cake. Who makes the time to run a spoof slander account?"

The doorbell interrupted our conversation. I tiptoed and squinted through the peephole. "Justin Woods is standing on our front porch."

"You gave the suspected murderer our home address?" Lois gasped. "Nice going."

"No." I curled my hair behind my ear and straightened my blouse. "I don't know how he found us."

He knocked. "You girls realize I can hear you, right?"

I cracked the door. "How did you find me?"

"I sweet-talked HR to sneak a peek at your info." He grinned. "Right call on the lawyer. Even the cheap variety I hired shredded the CBI's circumstantial case. But I expect they'll be back soon enough with more evidence."

I scanned the apartment and reluctantly waved him inside. "In the meantime, we've been looking into alternate suspects. Ashton Ashley, Vera Killgallen, and Barnett Sinclair are top contenders."

Lois plopped on the armchair. "We need another excuse to speak with them."

"Lucky I can take you somewhere to interview all three at once." Justin cocked his head. "I don't suppose you know how to tango?"

My two left feet buckled on my return trip to the couch. My cheeks reddened. "I'm an actress, maybe I can fake it."

15

A Swinging Time

The discount rack creaked as I searched for a suitable party gown in my price range. Budgetary constraints limited my options – princess pink prom costume or a too-tight, too-short little number.

"Pick something already." Lois threw back her head. "What about this shirt. Fancy if paired with a skirt or something."

"This getup is a dress. In theory. I'm even too tall to pull it off." I parted the squished clothing. "I can't throw on the first thing I find. I'm supposed to blend in with prominent country club people."

"I don't think you're going to discover anything suitable at the discount barn."

I sighed, knowing she was right. "I suppose I can buy something outside my price range and return it later."

"Stores tend to frown upon wearing returns."

"But it always works so well on television." As long as the tag didn't pop out for the villainous mean girl to spot and rip out with a snide remark.

On the other side of the mall, we entered an appropriate formal wear store. After another hour of searching and trying on clothes, I chose a flattering pleated A-line in jade chiffon. My credit card groaned at the two-hundred-dollar purchase. Shoes and accessories put me near my monthly limit.

"What about your outfit, Lo?"

"I can find what I need at home. The waiters wear slacks and crisp white shirts."

"Lucky."

"Yeah, poor Becky. Forced to attend a formal soiree with a handsome actor escort."

"The things we do to solve a murder."

As we split a mall pretzel, Lois and I discussed a game plan for the party. Divide, conquer, and probe.

The country club elite organized the shindig to celebrate the newest inducted member, Ashton Ashley. The soiree was the perfect storm of suspects. Everyone received an invitation - the stars of *Prime Suspect*, Ashton's friends, and other persons of interest.

Lois dipped her half of the pretzel in the nacho cheese. "I'm surprised no one revoked Justin's invite."

"Are you kidding? They live for this kind of gossip." I checked the time. "We better go. I still need to shower, curl my hair, and do my makeup."

I applied another layer of hairspray as curls cascaded down my back. "It sure takes a lot of effort to fake effortless hair."

Lorelai buried her head under my comforter. She spent the next several minutes attempting to dig a hole.

"Tough critic." I snagged my lip gloss and hustled into the living room. "Ready, Lois?"

She tapped her notebook. "Been ready for the last hour. Your ability to take forever amazes me."

"What are you working on?"

She flipped a page. "I'm outlining a series of questions. I want to be prepared. You are keenly aware I can't think on the spot."

I swiveled, tripping on the hem of my dress. "Do you know where I put my new shoes?"

"Kitchen."

"Naturally, where else would shoes go?" I gathered the sides of my skirt and hustled across the tiny apartment. My feet protested as I squeezed inside gold strap heels. "Place your bets now. Which comes first, blister or twisted ankle?"

"In the store, I thought you praised their comfortableness."

"I'm willing to call any shoe comfortable after hours of shopping. My numb feet couldn't tell the difference."

"The dress is way too long for you. Perhaps you can hide sneakers underneath."

I tossed a piece of tissue paper at Lois. "You're a grand help."

The doorbell rang and Lorelai charged the door. Justin stood on the other side dressed in a tuxedo. "You ladies ready?"

Lois grabbed her purse. "You're late, Hollywood."

"These parties never start on time. You don't want to arrive first."

"As a waitress, I probably should."

He snapped. "Fair point."

I ruffled Lorelai's ears and snagged my clutch. "Be right back." I turned and scrutinized Justin. "Nice tux."

"Thanks." He tugged on his cuff links.

"But I thought Lois is going undercover with the waitstaff. Are you joining her?"

"Pff. I look like Bond. James Bond." He held the door and waved me outside. "Careful on the steps, Tripper."

Justin drove a 2012 Mustang in candy-apple-red, a color matching his motorcycle. The former stuntman liked flashy, fast vehicles.

Lois crammed into the backseat. I smoothed my long dress and stumbled into the passenger seat. Justin closed the door and slipped behind the wheel. "So, what's the game plan?"

"We have three targets – Ashton Ashley, Vera Killgallen, and Barnett Sinclair." I ticked off the names on my fingers. "In addition to speaking with these three, we need to interview their friends and acquaintances. Be savvy with your questioning."

Inside the parking garage, the valet took our car. Lois offered a finger wave as she slipped through the service entrance with her 'borrowed' key card.

I hooked my arm through Justin's as we entered the Chalet on the Hill. A live swinging jazz band echoed across the grounds. "Ashton's taste in tunes surprises me. I expected popular tunes."

"Her aunt and the club hierarchy plan these shindigs," Justin whispered. "Ashton favors music so loud your chest hurts from the beat." He snagged hors d'oeuvre from a passing tray. "The food is usually top-notch. Care for meat and cheese on a stick?"

"Maybe later." I scanned the faces in the crowd, searching for our marks. "Hey, there's Barnett Sinclair."

Justin stuffed an entire appetizer in his mouth. "Let's go."

"I think I should speak to him alone. He's not your biggest fan."

"Fine. But hide your pocketbook around the weasel."

Of our three main suspects, Barnett looked least guilty. Though he exhibited a financial motive, his alibi and the physical evidence pointed to a female killer.

I touched the arm of his maroon tuxedo. "Mr. Sinclair?"

"Detective, I didn't expect you here." He waved at my dress. "You look beautiful."

"Thank you."

"Drink?"

"Can I ask a few follow-up questions, Mr. Sinclair?"

"Barnett." His shifty eyes scanned the crowd. "Is now the best time for this?"

"You want to catch your sister's killer, don't you?"

"Well of course, but this party is an escape. Ashton invited me as a tribute to my sis. I don't want to ruin her night."

"I'm surprised Ashton asked you to come."

He ran a hand along his frizzy hair pulled into a bun. "Why?"

"Well, everyone is in on the secret she and Maria staged their truce. I assumed your loyalty would be to your sister."

"I love Maria but I won't let a silly squabble interfere with my life. They were gracious enough to invite me. I'm not stupid enough not to attend."

Justin's comment stuck in my mind. "A place like this is perfect for networking."

"Fine. Yes. I'm guilty of being ambitious. I'm not pigheaded like the rest of my family and I'm not picky when it comes to investors." Barnett jutted his chin to a group of middle-aged men. "If you'll excuse me."

I craned my neck to Barnett's conversation with the whales and spent a few minutes reading their lips. Condolences to the brother, small talk, and finally shop talk. At the mention of investment, the whale's body language shifted.

"This is the last place I thought I would run into you." Sherry's voice cut through straight to my spine.

I cringed. "Howdy, boss."

She wore an elegant midnight blue gown. The bell-shaped sleeves flowed as she spoke. "You wouldn't be a party crasher, would you?"

My plans for talking to suspects and witnesses never included Sherry. I adapted my cover story and hoped to think on my feet. "No ma'am. I came with Justin."

"Woods is in attendance?" The surprise drew out a more pronounced Georgia accent. "Why would he bring you?"

I pursed my lips, unsure if she meant the comment as an insult. "Um..."

"Speaking to you always gives me a migraine." She grabbed a drink from a passing tray. "I guess his arrest stuck."

"You sound certain Justin is guilty. What about your wait and see speech yesterday?"

"Company line." Her eyes scanned the crowd. "How long have you known Mr. Woods?"

"Not long." Something about Sherry's demeanor put me on edge. I shook away the paranoia. "Really sweet of Ashton to dedicate this night to the memory of Maria."

"Yeah, the best of buds."

I faked surprise. "Were they not so close after all?"

"They dragged me in the middle of more than one argument."

"How so?"

Sherry's eyes narrowed. "Why don't you interrogate your boyfriend. I'm sure he knows more than me." She dropped her empty glass on a tray and engaged with familiar faces.

"Care for escargot?" I spun to face the terrible French accent.

"Hey, Lois. Learn anything?"

"Yes. Nothing gets rid of a mustard stain no matter how hard you scrub."

"Interesting." I rolled my eyes. "Anything relevant to the case?"

"Guest of honor is congregating near the front of the room with her entourage. I think the white-haired woman is Mrs. Killgallen."

I tiptoed but I still couldn't catch a glimpse of my mark. "I should find Justin. He probably has a better chance to talk to them."

"Some redheaded kid is talking his ear off."

I cut through the crowd to find Justin attempting to escape a conversation. The 'kid' as Lois described him edged closer to thirty. Freckles covered a prominent nose. "A few years before Ashton broke into stardom with *Mandy's Home*."

"Becky." Justin's face lit up when we made eye contact. "Excuse me, I promised my date a dance."

The nerdy fellow hung his head. "Sure. Sorry, I bored you."

"Who's he?" I whispered.

"Ashton's Fan club president."

I spun away from Justin. "I'm Becky."

He extended his hand. "Paul Marcus. I'm thrilled to be here with all the celebrities. Are you a movie star?"

I failed to cover a snort. "Far from it. I'm as low on the ladder to stardom as one can be."

Justin pinched his nose. "Paul, why don't you tell her the story about Ashton's rise to fame. I found the last half-hour particularly insightful."

I looped my arm around Hollywood before he escaped. Despite the heels, I barely reached his shoulder. "If it's as entertaining as you say, I'm sure you won't mind hearing the encore."

Paul beamed. "I'd be delighted. It all began with a curly-haired six-year-old girl. Cuter and more talented than Shirley Temple."

A middle-aged woman tentatively approached. "Paul? Ashton is posing for pictures with the fan club in ten minutes."

"Oh, wouldn't want to miss the hoopla." His cheeks reddened to the color of his hair. "This is Phyllis Montoya, the best entertainment blogger in the state."

Justin's eyebrows shot upward. "Blogger?"

The woman's short hair curled around her ears in a fashionable style. "He's exaggerating."

"Never. She wrote the perfect piece on our girl Ashton when *Prime* announced her casting. She's going to carry the show." Marcus spun on his shiny shoes. "No offense to you, Mr. Woods."

"What's the name of your blog, Mrs. Montoya?"

"*Showstoppers Exclusive.*" She added a flair of her hands. "My team excels at breaking the juiciest stories."

"That's where I remember the name." Justin pointed. "You reported my arrest before they slapped the cuffs on me."

She grinned, showing off expensive veneers. "Afraid so. No hard feelings, I hope. This is simply business."

"Sure, not like anyone's life is on the line." Justin shoved a hand in the pocket of his trousers. "How do you find your information?"

"Trade secret, I'm afraid." Phyllis locked her lips. "We better go, Paul."

"Good luck with the whole investigation mess. I know some fancy attorneys who could spring you like that." Paul snapped.

Justin tensed.

I gripped his arm. "You don't need crooked lawyers when you're innocent."

"Right." Paul touched his nose as if in on the secret.

"Why didn't you let me clobber the weasel?"

"Not really a fair fight, Woods. You two are on opposite spectrums of the weight class."

"Fine, you clobber him."

"How is your relationship with Sherry Newton?"

"Random question." He stopped in his tracks. "Alright. She's a competent associate producer. Organized, authoritative, strict."

"No bad blood between you?"

"Not on my end. She's ambitious and plays the politics game but to each his own. Why?"

"I spoke with her a few minutes ago. She's sold on your guilt. I wondered if you had a history of problems."

"Lots of people are convinced I killed my ex-girlfriend. Including you until recently."

"But with her ambition, Sherry should be interested in getting you back and keeping the show on track."

"The crowd is congregating around Ashton. Now's the time to speak with her aunt." Justin guided my elbow.

We cut through partygoers swaying to the band and approached the stage. I smiled as I connected with a friendly face. The swimmer who enjoyed Clark Gable movies was in attendance.

Justin cupped the woman's extended hand. "Good evening Mrs. Killgallen, this is Becky Robinson."

I masked my surprise. "We've already met."

16

Staged

My prepared questions zoomed out the window when I shook hands with Mrs. Killgallen. The woman I met the day I snuck into the country club. She shared no resemblance to her phony-baloney niece. Or perhaps she was better at pretending.

"Hello dear, I thought you worked at the club when we last encountered each other?"

I cleared my throat. "It didn't last."

"I see." She swiped white-blonde hair from the side of her forehead as realization dawned. "Were you by chance snooping for information when last we spoke? A reporter of sorts?"

"Amateur detective."

"Ah."

Justin's head bounced back and forth as if watching a tennis match. "I didn't realize you knew each other."

"Why don't you give us a moment to chat alone?" She shooed Justin and her many rings glinted in the spotlight. She sashayed through the crowd, offering greetings to friends. At an office door, she motioned for me to enter.

Expensive, eyesore art adorned the eggshell-white walls. I squinted at a painting wondering if the decorator hung the piece upside down.

I peeled my focus and zeroed in on my suspect. "I apologize for misleading you before. I didn't realize you are Ashton Ashley's aunt."

"I assumed as much. Why are you investigating Maria's death? I hear the police caught their man."

"You believe Justin is the killer?"

"I don't like to speculate. Reading mysteries doesn't make me Sherlock Holmes." Her voice reached a sing-song tone. "Knowing Maria, I'm sure there are plenty of viable suspects looking to take a whack at her."

"I'm surprised by your candor, Mrs. Killgallen."

"I abhor lip service. If I don't care for someone, they'll know where I stand."

My eyebrows shot. "Really?"

"You think I'm hypocritical? We don't choose our family, dear." Mrs. Killgallen approached a floor-length mirror and fluffed her hair. "With that in mind, ask your questions, Miss Detective."

"I hope you don't take offense, but can you account for your whereabouts the morning of Maria's death?"

"Home."

"Can anyone corroborate?"

"My husband but he can sleep through a marching band so I hesitate to call him an ironclad alibi."

"You didn't care for Maria?"

"Not one iota. I said as much the last time we spoke."

"You didn't go into details. Any particular reason you didn't play well together?"

"How long do you have?" Mrs. Killgallen diffused a breath. "The short of the story is her bad attitude. She waltzed into the club and made demands of the board. Each member carries a vote with veto power. As president my ballot is no more valuable than others. However, I expect a certain level of respect. Maria couldn't care less about tradition. She crafted side deals with members and bought their loyalty. She ostracized me from the club my family built."

"With Maria out of the picture, your problem disappears, yes?"

"Absolutely." She removed a tube of lipstick from her purse. "But I explored non-violent, more embarrassing strategies of removal. I wanted to ruin her."

I picked up the thread Ashton revealed the day before. "Your distaste sounds more personal. Did something other than normal Chalet business cause your issues?"

"Maria single-handedly blocked my niece's membership. Sighted disruptive tendencies as a reason to deny her application."

"But your family built the club. Who is she to keep Ashton out?"

"The smallest amount of power rushed to Maria's head. She lived for manipulating those in her life. This is why I can imagine Justin or anyone else is capable of killing her. She pushed people to the edge. Someone pushed back."

"With the club's election coming up, you risked losing your seat."

"I held this position since you wore diapers. I always run unopposed."

"Not this year. Chatter is Maria was poised to win."

"Useless gossip. They might fear Maria's penchant for uncovering dirty secrets but they would never turn on me."

"Her death solved a multitude of problems for you and Ashton."

"So it did. But I did nothing to spur along the process. She got off easy in my book."

I flipped a page in my journal. "When did you last speak to the victim?"

"The week before her demise. We argued about club business."

"What about your niece? She and Maria engaged in a public feud. Perhaps an argument went south..."

"Listen, I don't mind the questions directed at me. You're doing a job. But don't ask me to speculate about my Ashton. If you want to talk to her, be my guest." She gripped her formal black gloves and slapped them on her palm. "Anything else?"

"Who's your money on? If you read the story and played Sherlock, I mean?"

"A coworker is a reasonable assumption. Maria desired an extended stay, to be welcomed back for another season. She didn't care who she climbed on to reach the top." Mrs. Killgallen smoothed her lace dress. "If there is nothing further, I'm returning to the festivities." She swung open the office door and friends immediately flocked.

I hung back, pacing as I sorted the suspects. Each interview clouded my judgment. Every suspect's motive was as strong as the next. I hoped Lois or Justin had better luck.

The precarious high heels I insisted on wearing clicked the tiled hallway and my life flashed before my eyes. My ankle twisted in two different directions. Despite the straps, I sprang free of the death trap shoe and my arms flailed as I caught my balance. I straightened my dress and hoped no one witnessed the almost disaster.

Channeling someone with grace, I continued down the hall. Justin wore a path through an area rug. His crooked bowtie and disheveled spikey hair revealed his handling of the stressful situation. "What's the verdict?"

I clutched the sides of my dress and leaned my hip against an entryway table. "I'm not sure. This shotgun interview approach doesn't do much to narrow the suspect pool. Maybe we are looking at a *Murder on the Orient Express* scenario. Spoiler alert, all the passengers were in cahoots."

"I'm thinking about the blogger we met."

"Phyllis something? What about her?"

Justin adjusted his cufflinks, sterling silver in the shape of a U.S. Marshal badge. "I think the reason she's scooping stories is because of an inside source on the set. I want to figure out who's feeding her information."

"Murderer first. If we find the time, we can play gossip police."

"You think I'm paranoid."

I offered a partial smile. "I wouldn't phrase it that way. But you mentioned this leak idea before. I suppose I'm missing the issue. Don't most movies and shows deal with problems in the press? What makes this one more heinous?"

He stroked the back of his neck. "The intimacy of the articles. She broke the news of my arrest first."

"Indicating a rat in the CBI or police department."

"I reviewed her posts over the last month. More than half the stories revolve around drama on our show." Justin scrolled through the blog page. "She wrote about an argument Maria and I had on a closed set. Actors and essential personnel only."

"Any chance the boom mic operator has a big mouth? Do you think the leak is connected to the murder?"

"No clue but Maria valued her privacy. She liked to be in charge of other people's secrets. If she discovered someone on the set sold information about her Maria would make it her mission to ruin them."

"Which gives the person doing the leaking motive to keep her quiet." I bit my lower lip as I considered his pitch. "I agree the avenue is worth exploring. Especially since we're nowhere with other leads."

"Okay. So how do we go about finding the gossip source?"

"Right here. The party is full of people close to the show. Hey, and perhaps our investigation stirred the gossipmonger into action."

"You think Phyllis might meet with the leak tonight? Out in the open?"

"At an event where people are socializing. What's suspicious about a conversation?"

"True." Justin rotated his neck side to side. "I used to jump off buildings and wreck cars for a living. Yet the last few days made me redefine anxiety. My career and reputation are hanging by a thread."

"The cloud of suspicion is still hovering over me too. I'm highly motivated to help you find the real killer."

"Alright enough of my cry-baby-itous. Let's track down Phyllis."

"According to her Instagram, she last checked in at the buffet table."

Justin craned his neck at an artistic filter displaying the blogger's dinner. "How did people document their meals before camera phones?"

"They sketched a rendition and mailed it to their friends with a braggy message attached." I dropped my phone in my purse and muscled the clasp closed. Tiny clutches were cute but impractical with the growing size of smartphones and my OtterBox case.

We returned to the hullabaloo and scanned the dense crowd for the entertainment blogger. With the prevalence of the internet, every struggling actor/writer in Hollywood attempted to become the next Hedda Hopper. My short meeting with Phyllis and a scan of her site reminded me of the infamous columnist minus the outlandish hats.

"I don't see her."

"You searched for less than two seconds," I said with an eye roll.

"Patience young grasshopper."

"Too many people. We should split up."

"There!" I pointed to a woman slipping backstage and toting a plate of food.

Justin charged through the crowd. I struggled to keep pace in my death trap footwear. I shuffled into a run like Ell Woods from *Legally Blonde*, but less cute and more uncoordinated.

Hollywood jumped on stage without the aid of the steps and dipped behind the curtain. I pressed to catch up. Beyond the red velvet, he instituted an abrupt stop. No warning, no brake lights, I plowed straight into his back. He caught me by the shoulders and prevented a total wipeout.

With a finger to his mouth, he hushed me. "She's meeting someone."

"Boy, are we lucky or what?" My forehead crinkled. "Aside from the whole wrongly accused of murder thing."

Justin crouched, allowing me to bounce on my toes for a better view. Phyllis paced over sound wires and backstage equipment. But her secret rendezvous buddy refused to step into the light.

"We need to sneak closer. I can't hear a thing over the band."

I gulped. "Not wise. Any closer and she'll spot us."

Justin's jaw twitched. "What's the point of following her if we don't see or hear anything?"

I slapped his shoulder as the second person came into view. "Oh my goodness, she's Sherry. The dragon lady is the rabid blabbermouth."

"Hardly concrete proof. They could be talking about anything."

I squinted at the pair. "Phyllis asked something about a replacement."

"Do you have sonic hearing or something?"

"Shh. I'm reading lips."

"If you're reading lips, why does it matter if I'm quiet?"

The sly grin broke my concentration. "It's called focus, Hollywood." My gaze locked on the marks. "Sherry said 'no immediate plans'. Phyllis 'plans to recast Jake'." I froze. "Ooh, that's you... your character I mean."

Justin jutted his chin. "What did Sherry say?"

"Not sure. I guess you can read about it on her blog tomorrow." My posture straightened. "Sherry said something about me."

"You? Coffee runners aren't normally on her radar. At least by name."

"Trust me, not in a good way." I blinked as I struggled to focus over the vast distance. "Uh-oh."

"What?"

"Nothing."

"Your 'uh-oh' didn't sound like nothing."

I chewed my lip. "Nothing germane."

"Seriously? Is what she said terrible?"

I attempted to ward off the pink rising in my cheeks. "Nothing case related but uh, I guess gossip-worthy. Sherry thinks we're dating, you know since we came to the party together."

"Phew, I expected something worse."

I side-stepped reading into his words. "Now they're exchanging cash."

"Paying Sherry for the information."

"Nope. Other way around."

Justin edged from his crouch for a better view. "Why would Sherry feed insider details to a blogger and pay her to run the story."

"Maybe she's buying something else?"

"Hey, whatcha doing back here guys?"

I yelped at the sudden intrusion by the redhead fan club president. "Paul. Hi. We're uh..."

"Looking for her contact lens. She lost it." Justin's smooth lie did little to highlight his acting abilities. Then again, who was I to judge after a high-pitched squeal?

Paul attempted an awkward wink. "Ashton is calling all her co-stars to the stage for an impromptu Q and A with the fan club. I came back here to set up but luckily I found you, Mr. Woods." He curled horn-rimmed glasses around his ears. "Don't worry, pal I'll lob you a golf ball."

I hiked an eyebrow, attempting my best Vivian Leigh. I probably came out looking more like Groucho. "I think you mean, softball. As in an easy question?"

"Do I?" His prominent nose snorted. "Any who, catch you out there." He buttoned his bad prom jacket as he stomped backstage.

"I'm sure the club is dying to listen to me." Justin stroked his chin. "Do I qualify as a co-star anymore?"

Heels clicked as the clandestine meeting between the blogger and the associate producer ended. Sherry stopped in her tracks. "What are you two up to?"

"Ashton announced a Q and A for the actors on *Prime Suspect*. Justin is about to be mic'ed up." I resisted grinning at my quick cover.

Sherry's forehead crinkled. "She asked for you specifically?"

"I'm still part of the cast, aren't I?" Justin asked.

"For now." Sherry's critical eyes scanned for a few more beats. "I definitely don't recall casting you, Miss Roberson. You best be joining the audience where you belong."

I gathered the hem of my dress and exited stage left. Allowing my feet to rest, I leaned on a table and checked my phone.

Three texts from Lois:

17

Close Encounter

I plugged my ear and dialed Lois' number. The band finished their last song and the crowd offered thunderous applause. "Come on Lo. Answer me."

A finger tapped my shoulder. "Looking for me?"

"Why are you covered in flour?"

"Long story. But totally worth the mess." A beam reached the corner of her almond-shaped eyes. "We need to go somewhere quiet. I broke the case."

"Lead the way."

Lois dusted her slacks as we navigated the kitchen. She opened the door to the pantry. "Allow me to set the stage. The scene opens with a humble waitress in over her head. The angry head waiter orders our hero to retrieve additional baking supplies from the overstocked, poorly organized storeroom. Teetering on the top shelf is a fifty-pound sack of flour."

"Sounds like a snazzy clip for *America's Funniest Home Videos*, but how does this make you queen of the lab?"

"I'm getting to that." She panned her hands like a genuine director. "The door is cracked but no one is aware of the invisible waitress's presence. Enter Ashton Ashley in an elegant backless dress with beading and lace around the halter and a black and red ombre skirt. She assumes she is alone and makes a phone call to her expensive lawyer on retainer." Lois displayed her iPhone camera. "Like any halfway decent director, I caught the whole incriminating conversation on camera. Are you ready for the premiere?"

I threw my arms around her shoulders, flour and all. "Roll the tape."

"I missed the first part but I got plenty." Lois tapped the play button.

Ashton framed a hand on her hip and spun. "Riley, you aren't understanding me. Only a matter of time before the police find out. I need you to bury this. My career will be ruined.

"A credible source said they're testing the DNA under her fingernails." She migrated almost out of view. "Of course it is. She scratched me. I covered the mark with makeup but what does it matter now? I'm done." Ashton huffed. "No idiot, it's on file after you refused to make the DWI last year go away. I don't care what you do. Handle this."

Ashton hung up the phone and hurled a mixing bowl at the pantry. The door closed. The camera jostled. Everything went up in a puff of flour.

"I'll dedicate my Oscar to you." Lois pocketed the cell.

"Before you grow cocky, save the video to the cloud and e-mail me a copy. Justin too. If I learned anything from watching *24*, the last thing we need is for key evidence to disappear."

"Done."

"Let's present this to Cornwallis right away."

Lois tied back her hair. "Do you think he'll care? He isn't often receptive to the information you supply."

"Hard to ignore the smoking gun."

"I'll finish here and meet you in the parking garage."

"What do you need to finish?"

"Collecting my paycheck, duh."

"Did you forget no one hired you to work this shindig?"

"No, silver lining. They simply pay the people who showed up for catering. I'm not sure how legal the under the table dealing is, but I'm not turning down money."

"Alright. I'll find Justin."

I returned to the stage as the panel came to a close. Ashton maintained her composure and thanked everyone who attended. I waved as Justin fled. He untied his bow tie and unbuttoned the top of his shirt as if suffocated by the pressure.

"Here I thought you were a clip-on man."

His eyebrows knit together. "This is what separates my James Bond tux from the penguin suits waiters wear."

I shrugged. "They're all rentals."

"I bought mine, thank you." Justin wrung the tie. "Expensive pretending to be a successful actor."

"Or a struggling one." My smile slipped through. "Finally some good news tonight. We got the murderer flour handed... no what a terrible catchphrase. The killer is cooked. Yikes, way worse."

"What are you babbling about?"

"We need to go somewhere quiet so you can check your e-mail. While we wandered about the party following a nosy blogger, Lois solved the case."

Justin combed through his hair. "I can't believe Ashton killed her. I know they despised one another but murder?"

"From the temper flares I witnessed, she's capable." I pictured the dark figure fleeing the scene on my first day on set. "And she fits the general size of the person who bowled me over – big."

"Everyone's bigger than you."

"Not true."

"Kids don't count."

I held my tongue as we approached the valet. "My theater teacher in college said a shorty like me would never make it in Hollywood. I turned in a rebuttal titled: Hilary Duff, Kristen Bell, Judy Garland, Carrie Fisher, Reese Witherspoon."

Justin's mouth twisted. "That'll show him?"

"All short people under five-foot-two. They did just fine."

"I lie about my height to land normal roles."

"Really?"

"Yeah. Casting directors don't like anything over six-foot-two. Implications about framing scenes with those who are vertically challenged."

"I never thought of being too tall as problematic."

Justin leaned to examine the line. "This is ridiculous. I'll fetch the car myself. Be right back." He retrieved his car keys and tipped the valet anyway.

Despite the protest from my feet, I followed. "The walk won't kill me." But the steps to the second level parking structure almost did.

Justin clicked his fob, searching for the bright red vehicle. "Where is it?"

An iconic episode of *Seinfeld* popped into my mind. Hopefully, we had better luck than the gang on TV.

Tires screeched as an idiot whipped through the garage at speeds exceeding the five-mile-per-hour limit.

I spotted blinking lights. "Over here, Hollywood." I cut through a row and approached his car.

The screeching manic zoomed through the lane. I hesitated, afraid to cross paths.

Justin threw his hands. "Moron needs to slow down before he crashes into something."

We traversed the row and the angered driver reversed course. Brake lights illuminated as he fed the gas. I crossed my arms. "What's he doing?"

"Missed an open spot?"

The screeching tires reverberated in the concrete prison. He angled not for a free parking space but us. I jumped out of the way and Justin caught me around the waist. In a crazy stuntman maneuver, we rolled over the hood of a parked car as the manic crashed into a beam.

My heart pounded as I stared through tinted windows. The engine revved again. He backed up for a second attempt. We weaved through the rows but the pursuit continued.

"Hide." Justin shoved me in the back.

"What?"

"Go. Call the cops. He's after me, not you." Justin climbed on the hood of a Mercedes and leapfrogged to the roof of a Lexus. He whistled, drawing the driver's attention. Displaying years of training, he maneuvered from car to car as the driver dizzied.

I dialed 911 and gave a brief description of what transpired. When I hung up, I searched for a weapon. A section of the concrete structure crumbled into a brick-sized piece. Rhubarb protruded. No that's the pie, what was the rusty iron bar called? I clutched the brick and contemplated a plan. The driver continued to chase Justin. I followed the pursuit and positioned myself ahead of the car.

I loosened my throwing arm. The arm which helped my high school softball team win state when I gunned down the tying run attempting to steal second and get into scoring position. My teammates called me Pudge, as in Rodriguez.

The car spun around the corner and I fired. The brick twisted through the air and smashed through the windshield. But my plan wasn't without flaws. The driver dodged flying glass and accelerated.

I dove out of the way in the nick of time but I never caught a glimpse of the maniac.

Justin slid to my side. "What were you thinking?"

"I tried to bust through the tinted window. Between that and the covered plates, we have no clue who's trying to make you the next victim."

He helped me to my feet. "I think whatever we did tonight at the party ruffled a few feathers. They went from framing me to attempted murder. Something changed."

"If the lab matches the DNA to Ashton, the shoddy frame job comes crumbling down."

"Ashton can't parallel park much less drive like Steve McQueen."

"Maybe when she told her lawyer to take care of her mess, she meant to take care of you."

Sirens grew closer. Justin exhaled. "What do we tell the cops?"

"We report the insane driver and save the rest for Cornwallis." I checked my watch. "Way past his bedtime. We'll wait until morning."

Lois busted through the service door. Hands on hips she scowled. "Why do I always miss the excitement?"

18

HQ Inquisition

Six hours after the incident in the parking garage, I chugged a muddy cup of bitter coffee. Each sip puckered my lips but the assaulting beverage kept my eyes pried open. I spent the all-nighter cooped inside the police station answering questions, looking at lineups, and sitting with a sketch artist. No one understood the fact I never caught a glimpse of the maniac driver.

Cornwallis strolled in at quarter-past eight. He snagged a powdered doughnut, stuffed it in his mouth, and grabbed a second. "The fellas are, ah, telling me about an attack this morning."

"Last night after a party at the country club."

"Which club is this?"

I resisted the urge to throw my head back. "Chalet on the Hills, where Maria was an influential member."

"Kinda ritzy place for you."

"I'm aware."

Cornwallis displayed the artist's rendering. "He looks like a shifty one. Ever seen him before?"

On the insistence of the night-shift officers, I described the attacker to the best of my abilities. The leading inquisition produced a sketch favoring Agent Cornwallis. "Nope, but I'm sure he's a real psycho."

"He's the type, for sure." The agent pinched his chin. "Since you continued to duck my calls, I never got the chance to plug those holes in your story."

"Maybe this will help." I propped my phone on the desk and queued the incriminating video of Ashton Ashley.

Thin brows knit together after the clip finished. "What's this?"

"Probable cause."

"I ah." He hesitated. "Who is it?"

"Ashton Ashley on the line with a pricey lawyer. She's concerned about the DNA found under the murder victim's fingernails. She asks the guy to 'handle it'. Later Justin, the victim of a frame job, is chased down in a parking garage."

"And?"

"Are you messing with me?" Sure the agent was misguided and following the wrong leads, but I couldn't believe him too dense to follow the facts I laid out for him.

"My question, Miss Roberson, is what am I supposed to do with this? Illegal recording won't hold up. She'll say she rehearsed a scene or whatnot. Added to the fact you, a suspect, is providing key evidence." He shrugged. "I'll dig into this theory but you're not out of the woods."

"Why am I a legitimate suspect?"

"I can't say."

"You're wasting time, Cornwallis." I spun to the blocked integration room where they imprisoned Justin. "He's innocent and so am I. It's time to explore alternatives."

He crossed his arms. "Police work follows the evidence to suspects. Not the other way around."

"But sometimes the evidence obstructs the true picture unless you dig deeper."

"Tell me more about this automobile who chased you. Any chance this is an accident?"

"Yeah, that car is as innocent as Christine."

"Another supposed suspect? What happened to Ashton?"

"No Christine is the possessed Stephen King car... never mind. The driver targeted us. More specifically, Justin."

"Imagine a scenario, will you?" Cornwallis tapped a pencil on the desk. "Justin is presumed guilty by friends and relatives of the victim. But they see a killer free and clear, rubbing elbows and acting chummy with the society types. Overcome with grief and anger, they spot him again in the garage. Stricken by a need for justice, they gun the gas. Rage clouds judgment and they choose revenge. Which scenario sounds more plausible?"

"I'm fairly certain you don't want my answer." I sighed. "If you refuse to be open-minded about our guilt, I should consult my lawyer." My stomach sank as a familiar face exited the elevator. I ducked my head, hoping he wouldn't recognize me out of uniform.

"Ah Agent Cornwallis, just the man I wanted to find." Medical examiner, Dr. Eklund entered the squad room carrying a folder. He bowed his chin at me. "Officer."

Cornwallis reached for the document. "You working on a Sunday, Doc?"

"Results triumph fishing on the bay." He bounced on the toes of his sandals. "This one is a doozy."

"The DNA report?" The agent straightened. "I thought you said Roberson isn't in the system?"

"She's not. But our sample got a match to none other than Ashton Ashley." Dr. Eklund popped the collar of his crazy multi-patterned shirt. "Quite the surprise, eh?"

I couldn't hide the know-it-all beam. "Who'd a thunk it?"

"Aside from fingerprints on the murder weapon, no physical evidence points to Justin Woods. And being the bat is his, we expect prints." Eklund dropped the file. "This copy is yours, Agent. I'll be at the lake. If you need anything, ask tomorrow."

"How certain is this DNA match? Why is the actress in the system?"

"DWI last spring where she got a slap on the wrist. Bit a cop too but someone put the kibosh on the charges." He tapped my shoulder. "Can I steal a word before I leave?"

Wrinkles formed across Cornwallis' forehead. "You wanna talk to her?"

Eklund's eyes narrowed behind dollar store glasses. "Yeah. Is she busy or something?"

"Be my guest."

The men exchanged glances but miraculously didn't reveal my alter ego. I felt like Clark Kent as the doctor pulled me aside. "I need more of your excellent advice. The wife isn't pleased about my working on a Sunday."

"She should understand the pitstop before the lake."

"True." Eklund crossed his arms and rocked. "But she is not aware of the lake either. I told her I'm on call all weekend to avoid a child's birthday party. I'd rather spend the day with corpses than thirty six-year-olds."

"Thirty kindergarteners or people age thirty-six?"

"Kids."

"Gotcha."

"So, what do I tell the wife, Officer?"

"I'm not going to help you lie, Dr. Eklund. Maybe you should try to avoid any future trouble."

"Well let's assume I'm too tempted and make the wrong choice. How do I make sure she forgives me? Will the flower thing work again or does four times in a week lack creativity?"

"You got her the same flowers thrice already?"

"I put my foot in my mouth a lot."

"I suggest you help set up for your kid's party and if she doesn't need assistance, go to the lake and stay out of the way."

"Fantastic, I think I can spin that."

As he hopped into the elevator, I contemplated my 'Dear Becky' column. He might not write in if he uncovered my tangled web. Advice wasn't one of my strengths. Hopefully, I didn't destroy a marriage in the process of maintaining my precarious cop cover.

Agent Cornwallis leaned over the desk. "What's the deal there?"

"Fantasy Football question."

"I'm a soccer man myself." Cornwallis punted a Styrofoam cup down the hall.

"I figured as much." I propped an elbow on his work station. "So, are we hauling in Ashton Ashley?"

Turned out the 'we' was less me and more him. Cornwallis released Justin and me from the endless questioning and I called Lois for a ride.

"This is good news, Justin."

"I know."

"Your face didn't get the memo?"

The corner of his mouth tilted. "I'm waiting for the other shoe to drop. I won't believe this is over until I hear a confession."

I shoved a thumb at the station. "They're not much for sharing. We'll wait for Phyllis Montoya and the Showstopper blog."

"Something isn't connecting. Ashton isn't one to do the dirty work."

"What if she hired a hitman? You heard the video, though. She fought with Maria on the morning she died." I snapped my fingers. "Speaking of loose ends, Lois brought up some things you never explained."

"Did she now." Justin grinned. "I don't think she likes me much."

"What did you steal from the hidden safe in Maria's trailer?"

"An heirloom."

"You pinched a Sinclair heirloom? For what purpose, to pawn?"

"She kept a necklace and insurance papers in the safe. The jewelry belonged to my great-grandmother but M.J. refused to return it after we broke up. I didn't want to risk the item falling into police custody and Barnett Sinclair getting his grubby hands on it. Anything else?"

"Your keychain, the one matching Maria's."

"How did you..." His bottom lip protruded. "Never mind. What about it?"

"The cops didn't make the connection, but we spotted both halves of the keychain at the crime scene. Yours and Maria's."

He puffed a laugh. "She snatched it back during one of the many arguments leading to our split." He dangled the keys. "Ripped the thing right from the ring."

"More planted evidence?"

"You aren't turning your suspicions back on me, are you?"

"No. Simply connecting the dots. The keychain is a more personal touch to the frame job."

"I suppose. But a bunch of people knew about it. Ashton made fun of me on occasion."

The Z skidded to a stop as Lois entered the police lot going way too fast. "I worried when you didn't call. Since I didn't witness the excitement, they wouldn't let me stay or talk to anyone. Seems they might want to question the brilliant director of the confession tape, but no."

"Lucky you." I leaned my hip against the dusty car, afraid my exhausted body might collapse. I jerked from the metal as if sitting in the Texas sun and dusted the dress. No way to return it after my eventful night.

Justin slung the tuxedo jacket over his shoulder. "They locked us up all morning for never-ending questions. Didn't grasp we are the victims in the incident."

"The suspense is going to lead me to an early grave. Are you cleared? Did they arrest Ashton?"

I exchanged a glance with Justin. "Yes and no."

"Meaning what?"

Justin rubbed his growling stomach. "Can we play catch up over breakfast?"

"My mouth is watering for a stack of pancakes and hash browns. Do you think I can sub fries?"

I rolled my eyes and collapsed into the front seat. "You're a weirdo, Lo."

"I like fries."

"We better hurry." Justin checked his watch. "A staff meeting is scheduled on the set at ten."

My phone buzzed. "Positive spin is we don't need to rush breakfast. The negative, *Prime Suspect* is indefinitely shut down."

Despite the announcement, after eating and a change of clothes, we carpooled to the studio. Suffering from loneliness, I decided to bring Lorelai along. Perhaps I could sneak a play date with the star canine, Winston.

Justin lounged at his detective desk and tossed a ball into the air. "I'm not convinced this is over."

Lois stood at the murder board; dry-erase marker poised to write. "I want to construct a timeline."

Between the realistic police squad and the circumstances, I envisioned myself as an actual investigator. "Start with the time of death window, four to seven in the morning."

Lois drew the block of time in red and switched to green. "Ashton posted her yoga meditation thing at four and it lasted until almost five. You movie people keep strange hours."

"Early set calls," Justin said. "Where did she workout?"

I mapped the address. "Close enough to give her ample time to commit the murder. Even in L.A. traffic." Lorelai tugged on the rope I tied to my shoe. "Vera Killgallen claimed to be asleep and Barnett Sinclair's security showed him home all night."

Lois added the alibis, each in a different color. "Becky arrived on the set a few minutes before seven when she caught someone fleeing the scene." She popped the cap on the marker. "Which puts the murder window toward the end of our range."

"Assuming the murderer is the one who fled and not a scared intern." I hugged my knees and swiveled in the chair. "Why didn't anyone discover Ashton arrived on set early? If she fought with and killed Maria why didn't her alibi crumble sooner? Didn't she check-in at the security gate?"

"Morning guys are sometimes lax with protocol," Justin said. "They wave actors through without taking note. Wouldn't be hard to keep her name off the list if she wanted to."

"But did she?" Lois erased a name and rewrote the letters with neater penmanship. "Should we check? The logs might surprise us."

"I'm sure security will hand over their records if we ask nicely."

"Leave the distraction to me." Justin cracked his knuckles. "And Lorelai."

"What kind of scheme are you cooking?"

"You and Lois be ready to sneak into the security office." His feet smacked the artificial wood floor used to muffle footsteps for sound mixing purposes. "Here's the plan."

"Careful where you step, you're on my foot." I elbowed Lois in the side.

"Ouch. Are you trying to impale me?" She swatted at the thorny bushes outside the central security office. "And if you extract your clown feet out of my personal bubble, I won't be forced to stand on them."

I put a finger to my mouth. "Hush. You're going to blow our cover."

"As if the rustling racket we're making didn't already do us in?"

I parted the twigs for a visual on Justin. He gripped Lorelai's leash as he entered the office. His hands flailed as he made his phony report. Someone kidnapped... dognapped the well-trained show dog – Winston Hamilton III. The pretense provided the perfect excuse to spur the guards into action, and away from HQ.

"Coast is clear." Lois exploded from the bushes, leaving branches to smack me in the face.

I spewed a mouth full of berries and leaves. "You're like a herd of buffalo in confined spaces."

"The phony dognapping doesn't afford us a lifetime, Beckers. The last thing I want is to be caught snooping around security with two murder suspects."

We entered the office and each chose a section. Locked computers and no hacking skills left us searching for a hard copy of the logs. Did anyone print records anymore?

I flipped through pages on a clipboard. Nothing noteworthy. Filing cabinets and desk drawers proved equally unhelpful.

"Anything?" Lois asked.

"Nada." A crumpled paper under the table drew my eye. I dropped to the floor and army crawled to the scrap. Propped on my elbows, I unfolded the wad. Resistance revealed a glob of chewing gum. I hurled the paper. "Yuck." My head pounded underneath the wood and my vision blurred. Only I could sustain a concussion from Hubba-Bubba.

"Becky, your clumsiness saved the day, yet again."

"What?"

"I didn't think to check the computers. But this one is unlocked and only on a screen saver. You jostled the mouse and woke it up." Lois slid to the chair and selected various folders. "Where would you put visitor logs?"

"Are visitor logs the same as ID swipes?"

Lois shrugged. "I think I found it."

She scrolled to the date of the murder and I clicked 'ctrl p', the extent of my computer knowledge. A printer whirred to life and spit out reams of documents.

"Geez, how many people stopped by?" I snagged the last paper and used a binder clip to secure the pages.

Lois stuffed the packet in her purse. "Let's scram."

The bathroom door flung open. A security guard stood in the doorway, clipping his utility belt. The high-grade flashlight clattered to the ground. "Hey? What are you doing here?"

I yanked Lois by the arm. "Run."

Given adequate footwear and incentive, I left the klutzy problems behind and flat out flew. We fled the security office and busted into a prop warehouse.

I chanced a glance over my shoulder. The fit guard gained ground. "Why couldn't we draw Paul Blart for the chase instead of the Rock?"

"Less chatter, more running."

I lunged for the door and motioned Lois inside the prop house. The perfect storm of weapons and places to hide. "I'll hold him off, you make sure we don't lose the log."

"You're going to fight off the man you compared to Dwayne Johnson?"

I grabbed a two-by-four from the shelf. "Yup."

"Be careful." Lois jogged across the warehouse for the exit on the other side. She didn't need to know my weapon was crafted from Styrofoam.

The Pebble barreled to a stop and snarled. "Nowhere to run."

I swung the 'weapon' and connected with his midsection. The two-by-four squeaked like one of Lorelai's toys.

He laughed and clutched his side. He mimed my attempt to fight him. "You're a hilarious little pipsqueak."

I clenched a glass bottle. "Stay back."

He grinned and lunged. I popped him on the head eliciting no reaction from the breakaway bottle. I tried a second and a third.

"You're in a prop house." He grabbed a metal pipe. "This is rubber. The barbells are plastic. The knives are retractable. Silly plan, kid."

My hand fell on a frying pan. Probably molded from silicone. But the weight surprised me. "Don't be so cocky."

"What are you gonna do about it?"

I swung the cast iron skillet and grounded the pebble into gravel. He crashed to the floor, giving me enough time to disappear. I weaved through the studio and returned to the precinct set.

Justin propped his feet on the desk and held an ice cream cone for Lorelai. "Imagine our surprise when we found Winston in his trailer with his trainer."

I grasped my knees as I caught my breath. "Where's Lois?"

"With you?"

"I'm in the living room of Justin's character!" she called from the neighboring set.

I opened the squad room door and entered a New York apartment no police officer not on the take could afford. "Why are you in here?"

"Way more comfortable than the office chairs." She lounged on the couch and split the visitor log into three stacks. "Grab a stack and a highlighter."

I checked the first two names on my list. "Never mind. Hello smoking gun." I highlighted both. "Ashton Ashley arrived on the set at 5:47 and scanned her ID badge. At 5:50, Vera Killgallen signed in with a temporary visitor's pass."

"They were both here?" Lois asked.

Justin dropped to the couch. "They did it together."

19

Double Teamed

With a strong yank, I opened the jammed desk drawer. The workstation belonged to the grizzled, dirty cop in the station. I pushed aside a molded, half-eaten sandwich. "Props department went a tad overkill with all this junk."

Justin stabbed the prehistoric bread with a letter opener and maneuvered it to the garbage. "Can't blame props for this one, he's a slob."

Lorelai lunged for the expired lunch and I distracted her with a squeaker toy hurled across the set. "A method actor. Also known as a weirdo." I riffled through another drawer. "Don't any of these pretend cops use paper for note-taking?"

"What do you need the paper for?" Lois asked.

"I want to draw out our plan so we don't make any mistakes. The setup is delicate." I snagged a napkin and uncapped a pen. "Alright. To permanently close this case, we need a confession from either Mrs. Killgallen or Ashton Ashley."

"Because if left to Cornwallis, none of us will ever be free." Justin plopped on the worn leather sofa framing the waiting room of the detective squad. He tucked his arms under his head and stared at the false ceiling. "What if we re-enact the incident?"

I laughed. "Using all we learned? That'll take all of two minutes."

"You discovered plenty since the last time you visited the crime scene." Justin marched to a door. "I find acting a scenario out clarifies things you can't visualize on the two-dimensional page."

Lois swept her hands. "He's right. A different medium might spark an idea."

"I found Maria in the living room."

"The place we hung out all afternoon? Creepy."

"No. Another apartment set. The murder occurred in the star character's living room, not Justin's tiny flat." I tapped my thigh and whistled for my terrier puppy to follow. For a non-show dog, she picked up commands quickly. We entered the crime scene and an eerie chill swept through my body. From the moment I found Maria and called the police, time moved in slow motion. But I didn't remember the details, only the dragging uneasiness.

Lois spun as she examined the set. "They cleaned the area long ago, so where do we start?"

Justin gripped Lois by the shoulders. "You're Maria. Stand about here."

She gasped. "Why me? You can be the dead girl."

"You're the right size." Justin grabbed a throw pillow. "A stand-in for the baseball bat."

"I don't see any stilts, so I guess I'm Vera Killgallen rather than Ashton Ashley."

"Which one wielded the murder weapon?" Lois asked.

"Well, DNA confirms Ashton and Maria fought." Justin clutched the stand-in victim and she mimed a scratch to his neck.

"Mrs. Killgallen witnesses the fight, grabs the bat, and swings." I popped Lois in the head with the pillow.

"Ouch!"

I shook my head. "No dice."

Lois combed her long hair out of her face. "Well excuse me. I'm a director on the other side of the camera."

"I'm not critiquing your acting. The scenario is not right."

"I agree." Justin licked his lips. "This was planned. In defense of others, Killgallen would snatch this fire poker, a chair, or the coffee table book. She wouldn't run across the studio, break into my trailer, and steal my Louisville Slugger."

"What if we assume the killer, Ashton, lured Maria here to talk." I positioned Justin and Lois in front of the Styrofoam fireplace. "Mrs. Killgallen is waiting next door with the signed bat and a t-shirt she planned to wear. She hears the struggle and acts before she's ready. She swings the bat and smears blood on the shirt."

Lois crashed to the floor and opened one eye. "I buy the story."

"Killgallen makes a quick exit to hide the murder weapon at an area I frequent," Justin said.

Lorelai barked from her perch as if reminding us of her involvement. I motioned for my friends to follow. "At some point, my pup enters the set and chases the killer. Ashton. She sprints away from the crime scene as I enter the studio with morning coffee and bagels. Ashton bowls me over, leaving me to pick up the pieces."

"What about your ID badge?" Lois asked. "How did you lose it underneath the body? Did someone plant it or dumb luck?"

"In our scenario, the killers already left." Justin cracked his knuckles. "What if Ashton ran out first, with Killgallen left to clean the crime scene? She called her aunt after the fact."

My stride returned to the murder area. "I came through the squad room and took a few minutes to fangirl. I proceeded to the living room set. At first, I thought I interrupted filming. I didn't spot anyone else but the body captured most of my attention."

Justin scanned the room. "There are plenty of places to hide and multiple exits."

"Why do we assume Mrs. Killgallen stayed behind?" Lois crinkled her forehead.

"She's as tiny as Becky. She couldn't knock her over while running full-steam."

"The reenactment helped. Back to our plan." I took a seat on the couch. "We presume both women played a hand in the murder but one might turn on the other given proper incentive." I jotted down a bullet point.

"As bait, we send the same text message to each lady," Lois said. "Something to the effect of we know what you did."

A scene from *I Know What You Did Last Summer* entered my mind. "We should craft something specific so we don't sound like a maniac slayer with a hook for a hand."

Justin motioned for the pen. "You lied about your alibi and I uncovered proof you visited the set the morning of the murder. But we both know who the real killer is. The brains of the operation. If you want to keep Cornwallis off your scent, we need to work together."

"Why would either woman entertain a message from you?" Lois asked. "They framed you and possibly tried to run you over in their car."

Justin shrugged. "Self-preservation."

"If they think we're getting close, one of the women will turn on the other." I twisted my mouth. "Or make another attempt to silence you."

Lois popped her bubble gum. "What if they don't? Turn on each other, I mean."

"Worth a try to flush them out." Justin crossed his arms. "Are we doing this?"

"The case isn't going to solve itself," I agreed. "Especially with Cornwallis driving."

I paced the living room as the call went to voicemail. A few days earlier, I couldn't shake Agent Cornwallis. Now with the mystery partially cracked, he went radio silent.

Lois removed curly fries from the air fryer and Lorelai stood on her back legs for a better whiff. "Even if you can get ahold of him, he won't share an update on the case."

"If he picked up his phone, we could warn him about Vera Killgallen's involvement." I dropped my head to the kitchen counter. "Justin, any response from our suspects?"

"Not since you asked five minutes ago."

"Well excuse me for being anxious. But if someone sent me a text like that, I wouldn't wait a day and a half to act. Are you sure you used the right phone numbers?"

"Be patient." Justin opened the fridge and retrieved three cans of Dr Pepper.

In an attempt to calm my nerves, I ran through the case again. Which suspect would take the bait? Which women had more to lose? "The DNA under Ashton's fingernails puts her at the scene. What other physical evidence ties her to the murder?"

Lois shook her head. "Nothing else we found."

"And all we have on Killgallen is conjecture. She has a clear motive and opportunity but we can't link her to anything concrete." I scooped fries to a paper plate and squirted ketchup.

"If the ruse doesn't work, what about another interview?" Justin asked. "With her niece in the hot seat, she might be more willing to come clean."

"Don't count on it." I sighed. "Maybe we sneak into Ashton's trailer or home."

Lois snapped. "We can slip inside as cleaning crew."

I shook the notion. "Justin's right about being patient. We can't go snooping around her residence. Poor timing with her being in custody." A knock at the door disrupted our discussion. "Pizza's here. That was fast."

"My treat." Justin reached for his wallet and jogged to the door. He froze with a hand on the open door. "Guys its, not the pizza."

I craned my neck around the kitchen partition, lifting my barstool on two legs. The teetered chair sent me toppling to the linoleum floor. Ashton Ashley waltzed inside our living room. Expensive sunglasses parted her blonde hair and she cocked a hip. The text obviously didn't thrill her. But how did she trace the ruse to me? I hopped to my feet and dusted a scabbed elbow. "Did someone send a mass e-mail to the cast and crew, posting my home address?"

"Your little threatening message isn't half as clever as you think." The words stumbled through Ashton's teeth as she fought the almost compliment. "He can't tie his shoes without a script. Not difficult for us to trace the plan to his new girlfriend."

My neck stiffened. "Us?"

Justin cleared his throat and jerked his head to the ajar door. Vera Killgallen inspected the grime covering our entryway, acting as if someone crowned her the queen of England.

"What's going on?" Lois asked.

Ashton pointed a manicured finger. "Who's the extra?"

"Why are you here?" I asked.

"I must compliment your creativity." Mrs. Killgallen spread her arms. "For half a minute, I considered you might not be bluffing. Then I called my niece and she told a most fascinating story. Mr. Woods sent the exact same threat to her. Honestly, did you think we wouldn't talk?"

"From him, it isn't a leap to the nosy assistant." Ashton scrutinized the diplomas hanging on our bare walls. "You foolish girl, Justin blinded from the truth."

I shook my head. "We're long past buying the ridiculous frame job."

Mrs. Killgallen folded her hands. "We'll agree the scenario is unlikely. But the fact remains, you tried to turn me and my niece against each other. I don't take manipulation lightly."

Ashton eased to our lumpy couch and clutched her handbag across her lap. "The police are utterly clueless. They accused everyone who ever met Maria of killing her and refuse to listen to reason. First Justin, now me. My lawyers got bail but unless something changes, I'll be on trial for a crime I certainly didn't commit."

"Why doesn't your aunt confess and save us the trouble?" I asked.

"I beg your pardon?" Mrs. Killgallen ceased her scrutiny of the apartment to feign ignorance. "I am no more guilty than Ashton."

Justin's eyebrow arched and he crossed his arms. "A convincing argument if I ever heard one."

"Very cute, my dear boy. But you are off base."

"This is a waste of our time, Aunt Vera." Ashton slammed her purse against the coffee table. Lorelai barked and growled at the uninvited guest. "Shoo this mutt away from me."

I whistled and Lorelai hopped beside me. "Good dog."

"Your temper, Ashton dear, is what got us in this mess in the first place." Mrs. Killgallen closed the distance and touched my arm. "From our conversation at the club, I recognized your intelligence. Unlike the dimwit Cornwallis, you're interested in the truth."

"Who's truth?" I asked.

"I spent as much time speculating as the next busybody but rumors like this destroy reputations."

"The consequences of offing a person," Lois muttered.

"Aside from motive, why do any of you suspect my niece and me?"

"You lied. Both of you. Through your teeth." Justin pointed a finger at Ashton. "The frame job of me is a bonus. You get the show all to yourself."

Mrs. Killgallen waved her hand. "What are you accusing us of lying about?"

"Your alibi, for starters." I opened a drawer and grabbed the visitor logs. "You both visited the set the morning Maria died. Care to explain?"

"I told you someone would find out. And they aren't bluffing." Ashton huffed. "Why didn't the brilliant police investigator bust me on my alibi?"

"He doesn't know yet, does he?" Mrs. Killgallen's eyes sparkled.

Justin bounced on his tiptoes. "Newly discovered evidence."

"You need to share your side of the story and jump ahead of this. If you show good faith, the district attorney might be more lenient."

Mrs. Killgallen's head jerked to me. "A piece of paper proves nothing. It puts us at the scene, but Maria scratching Ashton already accomplished this."

"If you expect us to entertain your innocence, you need to try a heck of a lot harder." Justin cracked open his can of soda. "Did you accidentally break into my trailer, steal my bat, and hit Maria in self-defense? Then your aunt helped cover the crime?"

"You think you know it all. Don't you?" Ashton glared. "I fought with Maria the day she died. With her weak self-esteem, she couldn't take a simple critique. She scratched me and pulled my hair. I slapped her in the face. Even stevens."

"What happened next?" Lois asked.

"I stepped in the middle and offered a solution to our problems," Mrs. Killgallen explained.

"I'm sure your resolution was a home run."

Mrs. Killgallen's false eyelashes winked at me. "Clever, dear, but dead wrong. I'm going to tell you the same story the police chose to ignore. Not because of your ridiculous blackmail attempt or because I'm in any way interested in what you believe. I'm telling you this because we are innocent."

Despite my curiosity, I stood. "We aren't entertaining another tall tale."

Mrs. Killgallen waved her hand in the air. "What if I told you Sherry Newton is feeding inside information to the press?"

Justin slurped from his soda can. "Selling stories and killing someone are two different things."

"I never said the woman sold stories. Quite the opposite." The club busybody grinned. "Sherry is paying a journalist to print the information she wants. Her goal is publicity and to stir gossip on the set."

I shrugged. "And?"

"My dear, isn't the implication clear? Shady dealings such as this land you on the blacklist. Hollywood types value privacy. An insider trading in secrets for their personal advancement is at the very least, frowned upon. Ms. Newton wanted the show to suffer under the management of her boss. Her ambition won't allow her career to stop at the associate producer level. Problems on the set can be contrived through press leaks. Conveniently Sherry is always around to defuse the bombs and extinguish the fires. People in charge take note of those playing hero. She's riding the fast track to the top."

"She killed Maria to force a promotion?" Lois asked. "That's what you're going with?"

"Who's she and why is she talking?" Ashton flipped straight blonde locks over her shoulder. "Maria found out about Sherry's game and went for blood. The morning we fought, we realized we had a common enemy. Or rather Aunt Vera did."

"I offered to take care of her Sherry problem if Maria resigned from the club."

My forehead crinkled. "And she agreed?"

"Wholeheartedly." Mrs. Killgallen laughed. "Sherry is the one foe Maria couldn't best. An equal nemesis. Maria finally discovered dirt but she needed our help to implement a plan. We left the set with a deal in place and Maria alive and well. I fear Sherry found out and killed her."

"Why would Sherry want to frame me?" Justin asked.

Ashton rolled her eyes. "You're an easy mark."

"You were at one time Maria's confidant. A potential loose end.-" Mrs. Killgallen tugged her blazer tighter. "Given the truce with Maria, we don't possess a motive to kill her. Desperate people do desperate things. She would do whatever I asked of her."

"Says you." Justin shoved a hand through his hair. "You lied before. Why not now?"

"I don't care if you people think I'm innocent or guilty. What I do care about is my reputation. Your snooping carries a stench. Best I set you on the right path."

"Why didn't you mention Sherry before?" Lois asked.

"You're kidding right?" Ashton flipped a manicured hand. "We believed Justin killed her. Maria belittled him daily in front of the entire crew. I would have whacked her... if I were in his shoes."

I massaged the aching headache pulsing at my temple. "Mrs. Killgallen, did Maria possess proof Sherry leaked information to the press?"

"She confronted the blogger but I can't speak to any physical evidence."

I exchanged a look with Justin. "Is the blogger Phyllis Montoya?"

"She sounds vaguely familiar." Mrs. Killgallen pinched her fingers together. "Does this mean you'll drop this ridiculous pursuit of my niece and me?"

Justin snorted. "Not a chance."

"But we'll investigate the new angle."

"We will?" Lois croaked.

"The police aren't following every lead. Someone should."

Lois lowered her voice. "You want Sherry to be guilty because she's the dragon lady."

"Busted." I shrugged. "We will discuss a few things and dig deeper, Mrs. Killgallen. You may not like what we find."

"Don't worry, I'm hiring a team of investigators to clear us. You should look out, Miss Roberson, your fingerprints are all over this case."

In more ways than one.

20

To Be or Not To Be

I twirled car keys by the ring as we huddled under the car porch. The designated parking spot offered some shade from the harsh rays. A gust of wind sent the structure into fits, but the apartment complex refused to replace the rotting materials.

"Investigating Sherry is a waste of time." Lois positioned her hand to shield her eyes. "Ashton and Mrs. Killgallen are sending us on a wild goose chase."

"I'm not buying their innocence. But what's one day to be sure?" Justin asked. "We spend some time following Sherry and find out for sure."

"Lo, are you sure you can handle the search of Sherry's house alone?"

"In case you forgot, I'm the one who secured a behind the scenes confession."

"How can I when you remind me every two minutes?" I untangled a knot in Lorelai's leash and directed her to the car. "Everyone ready?"

"Frequent updates on Sherry's locale, Hollywood. I don't want her returning home and surprising me."

Justin slapped the visor of his motorcycle helmet. "I learned plenty of driving techniques as a stuntman. She won't lose me."

Lois slipped behind the wheel of Justin's borrowed Mustang while Lorelai and I claimed the Z. The temperamental old girl coughed and purred to life. The newly replaced air conditioning blasted and I cranked the radio, unimpressed with the selection of tunes. Was it too much for a country station to play actual country music? I couldn't blame California, anything mainstream gave me a headache these days.

When did I start sounding like my grandpa?

I chuckled. I could imagine far worse people to turn into than an old rodeo legend.

I cut the radio and focused on my mission. The three vehicles parted ways at the gate, each assigned an important piece of the puzzle.

According to the blogger's Instagram feed, she jogged on the beach every morning. I couldn't understand the need to share every aspect of your life online. Especially those already in the public eye. Weren't they begging for a stalker?

If I ever lucked out and became rich and famous, people would accuse me of being a modern-day Howard Hughes. Without the gross obsessions, of course.

From the passenger seat, Lorelai stared at the passing scenery. At a red light, I attempted to direct her attention to a squirrel darting across the park.

"I guess we can cross hunting dog off the list of former professions." My voice elicited a tail wag from my friend. "This role won't be a stretch of your imagination, Lorelai. Act cute and friendly. We want Ms. Montoya to be open and answer our questions"

I played the conversation and imagined scenarios as I parked at the beach. Did everywhere in California charge ridiculous fees to park? Or did locals keep a huge secret from tourists and yuppies like me?

As we marched through the sand, Lorelai tugged forcefully on the leash. She investigated every strange new scent with an excited curiosity unique to the canine family.

She barked as a jogger motored by. Although the word 'motor' might give him too much credit. With his pace, he wouldn't beat a tortoise in a foot race. The man turned and removed earbuds. Recognition flashed across his brow.

Lorelai continued to bark. I knelt to her level. "Relax. You don't need to chase him because he's running."

"Hey, I know you. You're Justin Wood's new girlfriend. We met at the party." Behind the sunglasses and sunscreen smeared on his nose, I recognized the nerdy Ashton Ashley fan club president. "Don't worry if your memory lapsed. Most of the pretty girls I meet don't remember me."

"Paul Marcus. The man with two first names."

He tapped his nose, smudging the lotion. "I freckle something fierce in the sun. Well, not entirely true. I burn and swell like the girl from *Charlie and the Chocolate* factory, but red."

"Violet."

"No, I turn a rich crimson."

"The character who swelled like a blueberry. Her name is Violet." I hesitated as my mind processed the odd coincidence. With a snap judgment, I leaned on my nerdy side. Far from a foreign role. "Funny to run into you here, Paul. Although, not super funny since several people at the party the other night mentioned this beach for exercise. Free from tourists and more of a local hotspot. Lorelai loves her morning stroll. She doesn't get near enough activity in the tiny apartment."

"She's a cute one. How old?"

"I'm not sure. She recently adopted me. The vet guesses under a year." I patted her head attempting to ease the anxiety caused by stopping the walk too soon. "I believe your friend Phyllis is the one who mentioned this beach. Thank her for me, next time you cross paths."

"You might spot her. We usually run together." Paul adjusted the sweatband slipping down his forehead. "I start first but I'm a slowpoke. She catches me in under ten minutes."

I faked a gasp. "Here I am blabbering like everything is peachy. How are you handling the news about Ashton? I'm sure the charges hit the fan club especially hard."

Paul crossed his skinny arms. The lack of pigmentation almost blinding. *He must be the palest person in the state.* "We're standing by our girl, like always. We genuinely believe this will blow over sooner rather than later. Anyone with the pleasure of knowing Ashton recognizes murder isn't in her heart."

"I tend to agree with you, Paul."

"You do? Are you coming around to your boyfriend's guilt?"

"I have someone else in mind entirely. I hoped to run into your friend Phyllis to discuss the matter."

He laughed. "For a moment there, I thought you meant to accuse her."

"Not presently." I winked. "Phyllis keeps her finger on the *Prime Suspect* pulse. I wanted to pick her brain."

He fished his phone from baggy basketball shorts. "Why don't I fire off a text and ask if we can meet?"

Sweat parted Phyllis' cropped hair as she reached into the fridge for a water. "Want one?"

"Yes, please." I caught the bottle and poured some into a collapsible bowl for Lorelai. "I appreciate you meeting with me."

"Paul said it is urgent. In this business, code for juicy."

"I bet you hear it all. Some of which never makes it to print."

Phyllis laughed, showing wrinkles around her eyes. "Nothing does these days. All about social media and an online presence. Luckily, I made the transition. Some of my colleagues clung to the newspaper too long and are less fortunate."

"Your stories on *Prime Suspect* especially intrigue me. Not only because of the recent news, but I work on set and you uncovered things I never dreamed of happening. The quarrels between Maria and the writers. Brilliant expose."

"Your flattery is embarrassing me. But much appreciated." The 'Showstoppers Exclusive' logo embroidered on the glass door, cast a shadow inside the office. Phyllis closed the blinds. "But I'm sure you had something specific in mind when you requested the meeting. Should I find my pen or is this a different kind of conference?"

"I wonder if you might help my investigation. Do you think Ashton Ashley is guilty?"

"Don't repeat this to Paul, because it would break his heart, but I'm not so sure anymore. I love the kid. She's talented and awesome with her fans but people wear a different face in the public eye. We never can tell who they are underneath the mask. Countless interviews left me crushed when important figures turned out to be another role."

"You think Ashton is capable of murder?"

"Anyone is capable. But she is predisposed to a short fuse. I wrote a piece after the Emmy's in, oh, the early 2000s. Something to the effect of another actress getting robbed of an award. Nothing major, simply my opinion. As a young child and the winner of the said category, Ashton spent the next several months attempting to discredit me. For one slightly negative remark. We since buried the hatchet, but the memory stuck with me."

The answer surprised me. Based on her slanted praise for the actress, I expected devotion. Her honesty threw me off balance. I cleared my throat and changed tactics before I lost all my momentum. "I think Ashton is innocent. Wrong place, wrong time. If she killed Maria, the act would be a crime of passion. Not a calculated frame job."

"Which leaves the boyfriend. Who else can it be?"

"Someone with their reputation on the line. I heard Maria discovered a leak on the set. Someone traded secrets to a blogger. Then your name kept popping up with the inside scoop."

"Is there an accusation in your statement?"

"Did Sherry Newton feed you information and pay you to print exaggerated stories?"

"I don't appreciate you questioning my integrity as a reporter. I spent more than twenty-five years in the business. Longer than you've been alive, I wager. I don't publish exaggerations or hyperbole. My readers demand the truth. Which is what I give them."

"But you don't deny Sherry as your inside source?"

"As a rule, I don't reveal the confidential nature of how I obtain gossip. But at the same time, I did nothing wrong. I write the articles people give me. Their ethical obligation isn't my concern."

"Hypothetically, let's say Sherry is your informant. And the conversation I witnessed the night of the country club party was her feeding you information about Justin's impending arrest." I perched my feet on the coffee table. The casual act turned out klutzy when my short legs failed to reach. "What if Maria discovered your secret alliance?"

"As I said, how I obtain my stories doesn't matter to my fans. If I bend a few laws or an ethical boundary for the truth, so be it."

"But Sherry has something to lose. Everything. An associate producer is feeding reports to the press to manipulate a promotion. That type of underhanded behavior is discouraged. Even more so than the standard backstabbing of our industry."

Phyllis covered a nervous hiccup. "You think Sherry orchestrated the murder? Oh my goodness. If that's the case, all of this is my fault."

"Did you talk to Maria before her death? Did she confront you about the leak on set?"

"Yes, she did. We engaged in a rather public argument when I refused to reveal my source. A week later, she claimed to find the proof she needed."

"Did you warn Sherry?"

"I'm afraid I did." Phyllis chewed her thumbnail. "Did I cause the poor girl's death?"

"What kind of evidence did Maria mean? Did she go into detail?"

"We remained careful but Sherry and I often met in person. Perhaps she followed us and took a picture as we exchanged cash?"

"Thank you for your time, Ms. Montoya."

"No thank you. This whole business is tying me in knots. I don't know who to trust anymore." She snapped her fingers. "Sherry is a meticulous record keeper. From the most mundane to the incredibly important. She might log our meetings, even if damaging. This could be the evidence Maria spoke of."

"Where does she keep these logs? Her computer?"

"Not something hackable. Check old school for something of this nature." Phyllis reached for her phone. "My daughter is calling. Anything else?"

"No. You gave me plenty to work with." I exited the office and called Lois.

"Hey, Beckers. I was about to text you a progress report."

"Are you still at Sherry's house?"

"Her husband bought the assistant picking up clothes excuse, but he interrupted my search way too soon."

"Did you find anything?"

"Nothing suspicious. I think we're barking up the wrong tree."

"You need to slip back inside her house. Apparently, she documented her meeting with the blogger. These logs might be the blackmail leading to Maria's death."

"If Maria kept the logs, where would they be? The police already searched for her house."

The flimsy reasoning bothered me, but not enough to abandon the idea. "Unless Sherry took them back. Or perhaps Maria hid the evidence at the studio. Somewhere the cops didn't search."

"A lot of conjecture, Becky. I feel like you're trying to make this round suspect peg fit into a square murderer hole."

"Interesting analogy, but I'm following the clues. Right now, my Spidey sense is pointing to Sherry. She, I can picture taking a baseball bat to someone's head. Ashton and Killgallen are the hands-off types. If they want someone killed, they would hire out the contract or opt for poison. A bloody frame job doesn't fit."

"Hmm." Lois hesitated. "A strong argument for a weak theory. Where does this leave us?"

"In desperate need for hard evidence. These suspects are spinning us around like tops. We need to improve by next time."

"Next time?" Lois balked. "You're expecting to put me through this homicide detective nonsense again? I don't think my heart can survive another adrenaline rush."

"You're right. I'm sure all the murders in Los Angeles will stop with this one."

"At the very least, I hope the murders you're implicated in will come to a halt."

"Funny." I nudged Lorelai in the direction of the car. "How about we meet at the set and see if we can find the log?"

"Talk about a needle in a haystack. We scoured her trailer. Where else would one hide evidence?"

An idea struck me. "What about evidence lockup?"

21

Evidently

I clutched Lorelai's leash in my left hand and used my other to scan my security badge at the gate. I shielded my face as the guard buzzed me through. Perhaps the goose egg on his noggin caused a spell of selective amnesia. My generic, girl-next-door face helped in some situations. He didn't recognize me as the girl who smacked him with a frying pan.

In my defense, I didn't expect a real cast iron skillet in a prop house. I merely tried to escape the Pebble's mammoth pursuit.

I met Lois outside the abandoned studio. Between Justin and Ashton's arrest and the police investigation, the show appeared caput. Just my luck. My first stab into the world of television was interrupted by a murder and the series gets the ax.

I shoved aside my self-pity to focus on the problem at hand. Lois crossed her arms, looking as skeptical as ever. Except for our only business class where the professor assigned teams to create and build a product using 3D print technology and the like. I came up with the idea for a board game, allowing us to use all the high-tech machinery A&M offered. Lois worried a board game went beyond the confines provided.

And here I thought developing a product included elements of creativity. Silly me.

"Hey, Lo. Someone steal your lunch money?"

"You say evidence locker and hang up. As if the clue is supposed to mean something profound." Her frown faded as Lorelai greeted her with a wag of her tail. "No kissing, puppy. Good dog." She finished the gesture with an awkward pat.

Apparently, in Lois' mind, licking was adjacent to biting.

"My statement is plenty clear. If Maria wanted to hide the logs, an entire precinct is at her disposal. The props department built an evidence locker, stacked with all kinds of goodies. A log would blend right in."

"Lead the way."

"You refuse to admit the brilliance of my discovery."

"If we happen to find the smoking gun in lockup, and your incredibly off the wall guess pans out, I'll wash the dishes for a week."

My eyebrows rose. "Why not a month if you're so certain?" I swung the cage and entered the chaotic storage. "I'll take this side."

"Why don't we check the box stashed by the door and labeled 'Sinclair' first?"

"Fine, if you want to break the carefully constructed search grid to look at the most obvious hiding place, be my guest."

The drop of Lois' jaw indicated her find. "You were right."

"What did you find?"

"A list of all the stories Sherry leaked to the blogger. Cataloged by date of the meeting. She also organized columns designating payment and the day the story went live. Her OCD record-keeping is going to destroy her career."

"And Maria knew it." I sucked in a breath. "Did Justin check-in recently?"

"No. I forgot to tell him I left Sherry's house." Lois punched out a text. "I wondered where he followed our prime suspect."

"Our? Now you flip-flopped to team *Dragon Lady is the Killer*?"

"I'm a bandwagon fan." Lois spread her arms. "Think this little book will interest Agent Cornwallis?"

"If we served up the murderer of JonBenét Ramsey on a silver platter, Cornwallis would shrug it off."

"Who?"

I threw back my head and my entire body followed suit. "Come on, Lo. Work with my pop culture references. She's the famous little beauty pageant girl. A notorious unsolved murder and the subject of numerous documentaries."

"Oh."

I shut the door to evidence lockup and we returned to the bullpen. "I think this book is our missing piece."

"The set is closed. What are you doing here?" The harsh words of the Georgia accent knocked me off balance. I spun to Sherry Newton aiming a Glock at us.

22

Hot Pursuit

My throat tightened as my eyes locked on the woman holding us at gunpoint. She asked a question but I couldn't think of an answer.

Justin did a swell job watching her.

"Nobody move." Sherry adjusted her grip on the weapon.

I swallowed the lump pressing on my vocal cords. "You don't want to do this. Shooting Lois and me won't solve your problems."

"Not another word. I know all about what you did and I'm putting a stop to it here and now."

Lois tugged on the sleeve of my sweater. "What now?"

I shrugged and lowered my voice. "For now, we do as she says."

"I warned you about talking." Sherry reinforced her hold on the Glock.

Despite limited knowledge of weaponry, I could certainly spot an amateur. Her posture and grip lacked conviction. Given the opportunity, we might stage an escape before her novice finger slipped and pulled the trigger.

Movement near the interrogation room drew my attention. Justin crouched, approaching Sherry from the rear. With silent steps, he edged into the bullpen. I averted my eyes, afraid I might blow his stealth tactics.

Sherry shifted and dropped her gaze to a pair of handcuffs. "Put these on." She slid the restraints across the floor.

"Which one of us?" I asked. "Her or me?"

"Your Asian friend first. Cuff her to the beam." Sherry motioned with the gun. "You, Becky, are coming with me."

I applied the cuffs to Lois and looped her arms around the pole. The slack would give her space to wiggle free. "Where are we going?"

"Nowhere until you secure your buddy. Doesn't take Houdini to escape from those."

Why did the bad guys always discover the hero left the handcuffs loose?

My jaw twitched as I complied with the order. Justin zeroed in on our captor. He lunged. I squealed. Sherry spun and fired two shots, inches from Justin's chest.

Time slowed as my pulse raced. Shock cemented me in place. With expanded eyes, Sherry tossed the pistol and ran for the exit. Lois cringed against the pole with her eyes closed. I slid next to Hollywood. The momentum from the gunshot threw him across the floor.

He dabbed his chest, searching for a bullet hole. "She fired blanks. With a prop gun."

My stomach somersaulted. "How did you end up on the ground-?"

"I dove." Without another word, he sprinted after our killer.

"Lois?"

"Go, go. I'll hang out here until someone finds a key to unlock me."

I raced outside, thankful for my pink sneakers. The perfect footwear for a hot pursuit. I squinted against the harsh sunshine and spotted Sherry as she hopped inside a studio golf cart. She hit the gas as Justin leaped for the railing. The jump came too late. He landed the leap with an athletic tuck and roll on the pavement.

I grabbed him by the arm. "More carts over here."

We sprinted to the cart hub. Justin slid behind the wheel of one while I claimed the second. His sputtered and traveled five feet before the battery died. I honked the toy horn. "Need a lift?"

With a slide across the hood, he swung into my car. "I'll drive."

"I'm a very good driver." I scooted after issuing the *Rainman* line. "She's headed for downtown New York."

Justin punched the gas and wind whipped through my hair. The gauge didn't reveal our traveling speed but it felt like eighty. He spun into a turn and the cart lifted on the right wheels. I gripped the railing as my stomach took a nosedive to my toes.

"Hey Siri, how fast can a golf cart go?"

"I'm sorry, I didn't get that. Can you try again?" the robotic voice answered.

"You are useless Siri."

"That's not nice, Beck-ee."

"Why does your phone speak with a British accent?" The stuntman showed off his skills as the cart sailed over a rickety bridge.

"Because when my robot annoys me with stupid, unhelpful answers, I want her to sound classy." I pointed at the horizon, a cheesy skyline backdrop used in studio tours. "There she is."

"I got her."

I reached for the megaphone rattling around on the floorboard. "Sherry Newton, pull over immediately." I jerked my head. "Oh, it's a voice changer."

"Yeah, I'm sure that'll do the trick. Now that she heard your voice, she'll come to a screeching halt and surrender."

I resisted the urge to try out my Darth Vader impression. "Simba, I am your father, Mufasa." Sorta.

Justin's green eyes narrowed. I prepared for a chastising. "How old are you?" He snatched the megaphone. "Breaker, breaker. Snowman, this is Bandit. What's your twenty?" He tossed the device over his shoulder. "Enough goofing off. Take the wheel."

"You mean pull over and change spots?"

"We're not going fast enough to be dangerous." Justin maneuvered to the back row of seats. "Stay on the gas before she makes it to the parking lot and we lose her."

"This is a bad idea."

"Trust me, I've done worse." Like a monkey, he swung on the outside of the cart and lifted himself to the roof.

"Turning. Hang on."

Sherry sped down a narrow Italian alleyway. The cobblestone path made for a bumpy, uncomfortable ride. Vines smacked the golf cart. I jerked the wheel to avoid the wicker table of a café set. The overcorrection sent us scraping into a brick wall.

As we burst through Little Italy, we returned to the wide-open spaces of a desert backlot. Justin poked his head over the edge. "I think you overstated your driving abilities."

"Only so much I can do in a toy car."

"At least drive closer to Sherry."

Sand caked the windshield as we circled to the old west set. "I think she's lost. We're traveling in circles."

Justin slid down the front of the cart and gripped the grill like Indiana Jones. "A little more."

Our high-speed chase cut through the middle of filming. Guys in black hats stood on one side of the street while lawmen patrolled the other. For the second time in ten minutes, people fired blanks at us.

Despite the phony bullets, each shot made me cower. I blocked the noise and focused on our mark. "Hang on."

"I'm not going anywhere. Take your time."

Sherry jerked her wheel to the left, dodging a rearing horse. The correction allowed me to close the distance. My front bumper nudged hers.

Justin soared through the air, landing on her roof with a plop. Sherry hit the brakes. Like from a bucking bronco, Justin flung off the golf cart. Unable to react, I smashed into Sherry's vehicle and sideswiped a trough filled with water.

Sherry kicked off her high heels and sprinted up the dirt road. I escaped my tipped golf cart and continued the chase. Justin dusted off and caught my shorter stride. We rounded the corner, approaching the studio entrance. We couldn't lose her in the parking lot.

I skidded to a stop. A dozen officers waited on the other side with their guns drawn. Amidst the crowd, I spotted Lois and Agent Cornwallis.

A smile spread across my face as I struggled for breath. We caught our perp. I didn't care we needed an assist. The grin faded as the actions of our killer surprised me.

Sherry ran straight into the sea of officers. "Help. They're trying to kill me."

23

Papa Bear

Cornwallis bounced his head from Sherry to me. "You people are at the center of everything. Every time I blink, Roberson, you're finding a new pickle."

"Sherry's lying. She held us at gunpoint, attempting to make us the next victims. We collected the proof you need."

"I... I... my patience for your shenanigans are shot. Enough playing investigator. Officers, cuff 'em all. We'll sort this mess out." Cornwallis tiptoed on his scuffed loafers. "You're not the only one who's been digging, Miss Roberson. I discovered some fascinating information to share with all of yous."

I shrugged away from the female cop grabbing my wrists. "No need for handcuffs, Corny. We'll come willingly."

Justin flinched. "We will?"

"After his spiel, we'll compare our findings."

Cornwallis motioned everyone to follow. "Let's make this conversation more private. The conference room is free."

I threw my arm over Lois' shoulder. "You okay?"

"Sorry for involving the CBI. I didn't expect him to treat everybody as killers."

"No worries. The truth will come out."

"It certainly will," Sherry said with a glare.

Uniformed officers opened the door to our dark studio. Paraded inside were a dozen people with connections to the case – Ashton Ashley, Vera Killgallen, Barnett Sinclair, one of the blondies from the country club, security guard Tarleton who helped me with my car trouble, fan club president Paul, scriptwriter Norv who Ashton berated, and Winston's dog trainer.

"What's with the reunion?" Justin asked.

Cornwallis motioned for the uniforms to cover the exits. "You might wonder why I asked all of you guys here today. A... a... odd collection of fellows. Well, one thing all of you got in common is proximity to our victim."

I slapped my forehead and leaned into Lois. "He thinks he's Sherlock Holmes."

"Between lying suspects and nosy buttinskis, the case spun us cops in every direction. So, I asked myself, *why is this situation so muddled. What's the common variable?*" Cornwallis snapped. "- Suddenly it hit me. The boys... and girls in the lab cross-referenced two lists. Guests at the country club banquet and visitors to the studio in the week leading to Maria Sinclair's death. All of you guys are interconnected. This fact led to my ah-ha moment."

"I am mistaken. He thinks he's Hercule Poirot."

"Who?" Justin squinted.

Lois shook her head. "Too obscure, Beckers. Explain."

"The detective from *Murder on the Orient Express.*"

Cornwallis slapped his head, reminiscent of the *Should've Had a Snapple* campaign. "A duh moment, you might say. You all did it, working in concert. Not a one of yous accomplishes this alone. The framing and misdirection and the alibis are all window dressing. You conspired to get Maria gone. Each of you has a personal stake and a role to play. You didn't count on someone attributing all the wackiness to a group killing spree." He pointed a thumb at his chest. "But you gotta wake up awful early to best me."

A brief silence lingered before murmurs erupted.

Sherry stood first. "Are you deranged?"

"I realize you are disappointed I figured out your little plan, but no need for name-calling ma'am."

"The conspiracy ends with those three." Sherry stabbed a finger at me. "Justin killed Maria. His new girlfriend attempted to clean the scene and pretended to discover the body. I don't figure how the Asian one fits, but she's an accomplice."

"Ridiculous." I rolled my eyes. "Why don't you tell Cornwallis about holding us at gunpoint?"

"I stopped a killer." Sherry spat the words with such conviction I almost believed her.

The blondie, Strawberry, pointed her head at Ashton. The star actress didn't take kindly to the accusation and resorted to a slap across blondie's cheek.

Cornwallis whistled. "Simmer down. I can't concentrate when you all talk together. If any of you comes clean, the D.A. is willing to propose a reduced and possibly suspended sentence in exchange for testifying against the others. The offer is only open for sixty minutes." He checked the timer on his phone. "These strapping officers are going to stand by and make sure you don't kill each other."

I blinked, attempting to follow his plan. "Is he secretly a genius? Is this a ruse to draw out the real killer?"

"How so?" Lois asked.

"Innocent people have no reason to confess. The guilty party might throw someone else under the bus to escape charges."

Justin shook his head. "I don't think Corny plans too far ahead."

I scanned the room. Some faces more familiar than others. "Interesting collection he assembled."

"Including all our suspects." Lois' gaze landed on each. "Are we certain about Sherry? Or are we back to another option?"

"Now is the perfect time to ask." I placed a hand on Sherry's shoulder.

"Don't touch me." She swatted my arm. "I am plenty aware of what you're capable of."

"You think we did it but I think you did. Which of us is right, Sherry?"

She crossed her arms. "My interest in discussing matters with you? Less than zero. Since you arrived, you brought nothing but trouble. Not a coincidence."

Lois produced the logbook from her purse. "Maria discovered your notes and threatened to go public. Your career in Hollywood was toast."

"The only thing lower than paparazzi is the people who leak info to them." Justin crossed his arms. "What, no denial?"

Sherry donned her reading glasses and snatched the book. "This isn't mine."

"Save it. This confirms you leaked the information."

"Fine, you caught me. I'm the leaker."

"That's a funny-sounding way to phrase it." Lois scrunched her nose.

"But I didn't keep a meticulous, damaging record. Never seen this before."

"Maria planned to use it to destroy your career." Justin pushed the book. "Giving you motive."

"First I am hearing of any of this. I am the only one around here who refused to treat her like royalty. Maria always claimed to have someone's ear or dirt to force my termination. And yet she was the one on her way out the door. She didn't need a push from me." Sherry folded her glasses. "I must admit, this is a creative way to fake your innocence. But I don't fool so easily."

I placed the packet in a manila envelope. "I bet Cornwallis will view this log differently."

"Not unless someone translates the gobbledygook for him. He hasn't mastered *See Spot Run*." Her perfectly shaped brows arched. "Why don't you go bug someone else?"

Justin scratched his head. "What now?"

"What if we strayed from Ashton and Mrs. Killgallen too soon?" Lois asked. "Their information on Sherry led us down the primrose path."

Despite the holes in Sherry's story, she didn't look good for the murder. Did my gut lead me astray with the actress and her aunt? Or was someone else in the room the killer?

Barnett Sinclair plopped his head on the table and closed his eyes. His body language said he lacked concern about a secret being revealed. Newt, Tarleton, and Winston's trainer never figured into my investigation. Did I make a mistake in not interviewing them?

I pushed the concerns aside. "We need to spark a conversation with Ashton and Killgallen."

Justin clutched the evidence against Sherry. "Go ahead. I want to pass the log off to Cornwallis. There's a chance he'll listen if it doesn't come from Becky."

Lois and I navigated the rows of suspects. The actress and her aunt huddled together.

Paul stood on the periphery, hovering over his idol. "Mighty chilly in here. Does anyone bring a cardigan they can spare?"

Strawberry threw her sweater. "Take it and shut up. I can't listen to another fifty minutes of you whining."

The canary yellow material tugged against his wider shoulders and the arms stopped four inches shy of the wrist. "Much appreciated." To his disappointment, Ashton never acknowledged his presence.

Mrs. Killgallen's icy stare scrutinized my appearance. "You did a fine job of muffing the investigation. Agent Cornwallis is so far off the scent he needs a seeing-eye dog to find the trail."

I sat on the edge of the table. "You two need a road map to follow your web of lies. So, I think you should watch where you cast stones."

"What did you say to Sherry?" Ashton asked. "We caught you talking to her."

"I don't think she's behind the murder."

"Our private investigator begs to differ."

Mrs. Killgallen placed a hand on her niece. "Now is not the time, my dear. Remain calm and don't allow them to rile your temper."

I twisted my mouth and twirled to Lois. "I think Vera might be questioning her niece's innocence."

"Quit trying to drive a wedge, you little troll."

"Ashton!" Mrs. Killgallen pinched her nose. "You're giving me a migraine."

Paul popped into the conversation. "I have aspirin." He unzipped a fanny pack. "I always carry meds on my person, just in case. You never can guess when there might be an allergy attack or worse." He rifled through the contents, spilling a few prescription bottles in the process. The labels with unpronounceable names piqued my interest.

Mrs. Killgallen accepted the Advil. "Thank you, dear."

"Glad to help." A smile spread to Paul's eyes. "After Agent Cornwallis releases us, we can all go out for lunch. What do you think, Ashton?"

"I don't think so, Pete. I lost my appetite."

"You silly goose, I'm Paul." He shoved the sleeves of the borrowed sweater. "Everyone's got to eat. You can, everybody can stop by my house and I will make sandwiches. It's really no bother."

Tarleton waded into the conversation. "I never turn my nose up to a free meal. Especially is if Ashton's coming."

She flashed a smile. "I apologize for my bit of the grumps. I'm delighted to attend."

Paul's eyes danced from the security guard to his idol. "Excellent. The more the merrier."

"I think we'll pass." I grabbed Lois' arm. "Did you catch that?"

"What?"

"You're so oblivious sometimes."

"Don't tell me, you're switching suspects again."

"Part of the investigation process. Rick Castle never got it right on the first guess."

The door burst open and Cornwallis bustled inside. He rubbed his hands together, grinning like a possum. "Who's ready to spill their guts?"

Despite a clever ruse, the killer did not attempt to strike a deal with Cornwallis. After more questioning, he relented to our release.

My mind spun with new scenarios. But I didn't want to voice my theories until I collected more evidence. I already received enough grief for my wild guesses.

"Corny took the log but he didn't show interest in the *Sherry acted alone* theory." Justin combed his hair. "What now?"

Lois punched his shoulder

"Ouch. Why did you clobber me?"

"Leading Sherry straight to us. What happened to watching her?" Lois asked.

"I did. My job was to keep her out of the house. How am I supposed to know you two broke mission and returned to the studio?" Justin sighed. "Why are you so quiet, Becky?"

A text message illuminated my phone screen.

"Who's texting you?" Lois asked.

"Papa Beau."

Justin frowned. "Who's papa bear?"

"Not bear, Beau. My grandfather."

"He's the number one fan of *Prime Suspect*," I explained. "But he doubts my tales about the adventures."

"I'll pose for a selfie with you," Justin offered.

"Let me send the picture of the set first."

I scrolled through my numerous photos of Lorelai – sporting her new collar, playing with a new toy, first visit to the park. How did I find space on my phone for more?

My thumb clicked the goofy selfie snapped on my first day. The smile of a girl with hopes. Back when I fantasized about turning my gopher job into a starring role. Before I discovered the body and became a real prime suspect.

My brow crinkled. I zoomed the photograph and adjusted the brightness. "Oh my goodness. Papa Beau solved the case."

24

The Smoking Bat

I selected a tub of potato salad from the premade deli section. "Not Rachel Ray approved, but better than arriving empty-handed."

"Are we sure this isn't another red herring?" Lois asked. "We've been certain about suspects before."

"Sorta hard to mistake him for the killer when's holding a blood-stained baseball bat." Justin dropped a pie into the shopping cart.

I zoomed in on the selfie. How did I miss a murderer lurking in the background? If only I checked the picture earlier. "This alone might be enough for an arrest, but I prefer to present all the evidence we can to Cornwallis. A confession would be ideal."

After discovering the photo, we accepted Paul Marcus' lunch invitation. As we headed to the house, we put a plan in place to trap the killer.

After a ring of the bell, we entered a Spanish style adobe. Framed photographs of celebrities and musicians covered the walls. Paul devoted an exclusive shrine to Ashton Ashley.

"Cool pictures." I pointed to a group photo. "Where's this?"

Paul beamed. "From our fan club trip two years ago. We went to Vegas for a conference. Ashton showed up and surprised everyone. It was the first time we met."

Justin traced the collection. "Hey, a section of your timeline is missing. What happened four years ago?"

A rosy cheek twitched. "Nothing. Preferences change. Sometimes you meet your favorite actress and they turn out to be an entirely different person."

"But with Ashton, what you see is what you get, right?" I resisted the urge to add an eye roll.

"Absolutely. One of the most genuine people I ever met." He motioned to our bags. "You didn't need to bring anything but I appreciate the thought. I'll drop them in the kitchen. The gang is in the formal dining room."

Ashton sat on the couch next to the security guard, Tarleton. She twirled her hair as he spoke about surfing exploits and his rock band. Mrs. Killgallen hovered nearby, keeping her niece out of trouble. None of the other suspects took advantage of Paul's offer.

"What are you guys doing here?" Ashton asked. "Trying to spoil another party?"

"Here for the sandwiches." Justin propped an elbow on the mantle. "What about you, Ashton."

"Pablo is sweet enough to invite us and my fans are the best in the world. This is my chance to give back and show how much I care."

Tarleton leaned closer. "Paul."

"Huh? What did I say?"

The swinging patrician burst open. Paul wielded a cleaver at the entryway. "Dinner is served."

Lois exchanged a glance with me. "Becky?"

"Danger Rebecca Robinson."

"Just what we need," Justin muttered.

"Everyone take your seat and I'll bring in the tray of delicious sandwiches."

Tarleton held a chair out for Ashton and maneuvered beside her. Paul swept in and snagged the seat. "I always sit in my spot. How about you go on the other side, okay pal?"

"Whatever dude."

I followed his retreating steps and poked my head into the kitchen. "Need any help, Paul?"

"No, no." He balanced four plates and placed them in front of each girl. He returned for the final two for Justin and Tarleton. "I added a special ingredient. Hope you boys enjoy."

"I'm starved but..." Justin stabbed his bread as the fan club president bustled back to the kitchen. "Any chance he's trying to poison me and the guy making time with his girl? I don't like the 'special ingredient' crack."

I opened the seal on the potato salad and scooped him a healthy helping. "Maybe stick to this."

Lois cut her sandwich into pieces and hid some in her napkin. "You better make your break now, Becky. We'll distract him."

"What are you guys whispering about?" Ashton's loud tone alerted everyone in the vicinity.

Vera Killgallen's eyes locked with mine. "Relax, my dear. You are starting to sound paranoid. They are enjoying this meal, same as us."

Paul popped up beside me. "Where are you going?"

"I need to wash up. Where's your bathroom?"

"Down the hall on the right. Hurry back."

I flashed a thumbs up and scurried through the entryway. With a glance over my shoulder, I made a sharp turn upstairs. More photographs littered his walls. Framed magazine spreads of Ashton Ashley and a *TV Guide* cover from her child star days rounded out the collection.

With an ear-piercing creak, I opened a bedroom door. A boring, tidy guest room. I continued down the hall to the master. Again, nothing stood out of place - a crisply made bed up to Army standards, a color-coded closet, and drawers of perfectly folded laundry. "Does Sheldon Cooper live here?"

I closed off the room and set my sites on a triangular-shaped wooden door leading to the attic. The simple tumbler proved no match for my lock-picking abilities.

Tiny steps led to a small office with a pitched ceiling. Someone taller might worry about smacking their head on the exposed beams. Candid shots of Ashton Ashley at Yoga class, in her car, and arriving at the set littered the desk. All snapped from the required stalker distance.

I kicked at the basin in the corner of the room. Ashes. I sniffed the remnants. Not from wood or a cigarette. It reeked of burned paper. I sifted through the debris until I found something not entirely charred. I wiped the soot with a rag.

A younger, pimple-faced Paul Marcus stood in line at a Comic-Con convention. Posing with him was non-other than Maria Sinclair. Additional charred papers mentioned the Sinclair Super Supporters. The Ashton Ashley fan club wasn't Paul's first reign as president.

I gulped as his motive became clearer. Spurned by Maria, Paul switched fandoms. The feud between the actresses reignited his hatred. I snapped pictures of all the evidence.

Footsteps on the stairs sent my pulse into overdrive. I returned the items and cut the lights. I bounded downstairs and smacked into Justin.

He gripped me by the waist, preventing a spill. "What's taking so long? Find anything in the attic?"

"Sort of. I'll go into detail later. We better hurry back."

An 11x17 frame drew my attention. Hand-painted letters adorned the plastic 'MOM'. "Recognize her?"

"Is she Paul's mother?"

I added the photo to my evidence album. "She's been covering for him this whole time."

"Hey, did y'all get lost?" Lois' voice carried with an unnatural volume. "Paul and I are looking for you."

With a deep breath, I stepped into a role. I played the part of a detective not intimidated by the creepy killer who caught us snooping. "Hi, Paul. I apologize for getting sidetracked. I am marveling at your collection. You possess an excellent eye. Very impressive."

A smile tilted, reaching his eyes. "Most people think my hobby odd. My decorator had the audacity to say these many photos overpower a room."

"Not at all. They are a conversation starter. Did Ashton see these yet?"

"No. I planned to give a tour after the meal." He motioned to the stairs. "Shall we?"

Justin bounced downstairs as Lois lingered. "What did you learn?"

"Mommy Dearest, Phyllis Montoya, has some 'splaining to do."

Lois covered her cheeks like the frightened emoji face. "His mother is the blogger?"

25

Follow the iPhone

With a running start, Justin punted the trash bin across the station. "How dense are you?"

"Settle down before I slap the cuffs on you again." Cornwallis massaged his migraine. "You kids are making me out like an idiot on this case. Your investigation is confusing me and messing with my flow. No...no one can work under these conditions"

I bottled my frustration. "We brought you evidence on the killer."

"Served on a silver platter," Justin added. "What more do you need?"

"I can't make an arrest on what you told me. I can bring him in for questioning if I'm so inclined."

"You put him in a room without charges and you'll learn nothing," Justin said. "Paul thinks he fooled everyone. You need to show him who's boss."

"I'm not jumping into another hasty decision."

Lois attempted to defuse the tension. "What can we do to help? What do you need for an arrest?"

"Evidence. A confession." Cornwallis shrugged. "The things us cops need before we go making accusations."

"Can you at least dig for a connection between Maria and Paul?" I tapped his computer monitor. "We're thinking he stalked her a few years ago."

"Fine." Cornwallis sighed as he used a two-finger approach on his keyboard. "Nada."

"You put Maria *Saintclair* instead of *Sinclair*." I gently nudged Cornwallis aside to type the correct name.

"Thanks for the assist, Roberson." He clicked a few buttons. "Ah, this is interesting."

"What?"

Cornwallis dug through trash and papers for reading glasses. "The vic took out a restraining order three years ago on a Mr. Paul Marcus. If this happens to be the same fellow, you might be on to something."

I pointed to the driver's license. "One and the same."

"I'll rustle up the suspect and bring him in." Cornwallis rubbed his hands together. "You kids go home. Thanks for the assist."

Instead of going home, we waited around the station. Cornwallis and company interviewed Paul for five hours. From what we gathered, not once did he request counsel.

"Paul's running laps in Corny's head." Justin tussled his hair.

"Paul knows the evidence is circumstantial. All we have are a few photographs."

"One placing him at the murder scene," Lois said.

I shook my head. "Doesn't take an expert defense attorney to throw in reasonable doubt. Ashton's DNA under the fingernails is the perfect out."

"What about Phyllis?" Justin asked.

"She might be an avenue worth exploring." I stroked my chin. "She all but threw Ashton under the bus before I presented Sherry as an alternative suspect. She might be protecting her son, but she doesn't share the Ashton obsession."

Lois' eyes widened. "Is he sloppy enough to call her after the murder to help him clean up?"

"We need to check her phone." I glanced around the precinct. "I'm surprised she didn't show up to support her boy."

Justin spread his arms. "Hey, I don't think anybody told her."

"Maybe we should give her a buzz." I whipped out my cell and dialed the number on her business card. "Hello Phyllis, this Becky Robinson. Paul asked me to call you if things got out of hand."

"Call me, why?"

She fished for how much I knew about the situation. "You appear to be one of his closest friends. The police hauled him down to the station. New evidence came in and they think he participated in the murder."

"I'm on my way."

I placed the phone face down on the desk. "Now she's coming to us."

The concerned mama bear arrived in record time given limited traffic in the wee hours of the morning. "Where's Paul?" She dropped her handbag on the filing cabinet, her iPhone protruding from a pocket.

Justin guided her arm. "I'll take you to him." He sent a wink back to us. The plan was on.

I snagged the phone and a lock screen greeted me. "Guessing the pin is a lousy option. Any ideas?"

"Don't look at me." Lois spread her arms. "I'm terrible with anything hacking adjacent."

The lightbulb went off. "I'm friends with a hacker back home in Lake Falls. Hopefully, she isn't too busy to answer."

Lois leaned over my shoulder. "Shouldn't you provide context so she doesn't think you're up to something fishy or illegal?"

"No, Samantha abhors small talk. We worked together forever. She trusts me."

My phone buzzed.

Unsure what she meant, I took a shot.

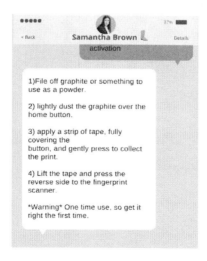

Lois collected the supplies and I followed the instructions to a T. Within minutes, we hacked Phyllis' device like a couple of real spies.

"None of her text messages predate last week."

"Awesome." Lois frowned. "Can we retrieve deleted texts?"

"Let me consult the Nerd Herd again."

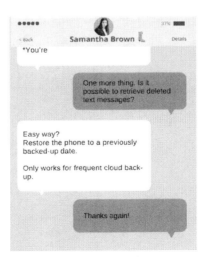

I spent a few beats searching for the cloud stuff before eventually locating the screen I needed. The phone was last backed-up the day

of the murder. Perfect. I started the restoration process and the next screen taunted me.

"You got to be kidding."

"What now?" Lois asked.

"You need a passcode to reset."

"Not the finger thing?"

"Nope. How are we going to bypass this?"

"Can your friend help again?"

Unwilling to admit my stupidity, I tried something off the wall first. "I'm always forgetting passwords and whatnot. I don't do this anymore because it's dumb and not safe, but I used to write them in a note. Phyllis might do the same?" I scrolled through dozens of notes – recipes, passwords, shopping lists. I hit paydirt on the first note created. Her four-digit passcode. My thumbs flew across the screen as I reset the phone.

"She's coming back."

"Now? You're kidding?"

"What do we do?" Lois' voice cracked.

I snatched the purse and fled. "Tell her I mistakenly grabbed the wrong bag on the way to the ladies room. Hopefully, this buys us enough time."

"Go. I'll do my best to bluff."

I slipped to the bathroom and checked the progress bar. "Seriously? Ten percent?"

The door creaked open and I scurried inside a stall. I stood on the toilet so my feet wouldn't show underneath.

"Becky? Are you in here? I need my purse."

At the sound of her voice, my foot splashed in the blue water. *Gross.* "Your purse?"

"Are you okay?"

"Yeah. Give me a second." I pounded on the toilet paper dispenser, distracting her with sounds.

"Slide my bag under. I am in a hurry."

"I can't reach. I'll just be a moment."

The progress bar reached the end and the Apple logo appeared. I typed the passcode and opened her text messages. With my phone, I recorded a video as I scrolled through her exchange with Paul. Before I thought better, I deleted the thread which revealed my snooping. I returned the iPhone to the purse and flushed.

"Sorry, I have a bag like this at home. I mistakenly grabbed yours out of habit."

"I didn't take you for a Birkin customer. They are quite pricey."

"Mines a knockoff." I filled the silence with nervous laughter and washed my hands. "How's Paul?"

"On his way home. This Cornwallis character is off his rocker with the accusations." She offered a smile. "Thank you for calling me."

"No problem. I'm glad everything turned out okay."

Phyllis exited the bathroom and I couldn't wait any longer to read the thread of messages. The first one on the list said enough.

Mom, I didn't listen. I did something terrible.

26

A Ruse

Cornwallis buttoned his cheap suit jacket and smoothed the wrinkled material. "I... I can't understand how you persuaded the brass to participate in something so... ah... utterly ridiculous. You're civilians for goodness sakes."

A female officer positioned a recording transmitter thing on my back and ran the cable up the back of my blouse. I wasn't well-versed in the technical jargon, but the wire recorded the confession.

"I don't need her tagging along." Ashton Ashley flipped her hair. "I'm plenty capable."

"The captain disagreed." I bit my lip, attempting an approach to not alienate my undercover ally. "Paul trusts you. He'll do anything you say. But I can sell the story because of my involvement in the case."

Lois nudged my arm. "Are you sure about this, Becky?"

No. "Yes. Y'all are only a code phrase away."

Justin circled his wrist. "Repeat the mantra."

I rolled my eyes. "When I say 'pineapple' Cornwallis and the uniforms will come busting into Paul's house."

"You clear on what we need?" Cornwallis asked.

"A full confession and explanation are ideal." I shrugged into a jean jacket, obscuring the wire.

"But don't put yourselves in harm's way on account of a total admission," Cornwallis said. "The text message exchange is enough to make an arrest."

"An admission ensures a conviction."

"I can't believe this psycho is president of my fan club." Ashton cringed. "You don't think he would turn on me, do you?"

"Follow my lead and you'll be fine."

Justin stretched his back. "I should come with you."

"Not a chance." I shook my head. "Paul's threatened by you. He will clam up."

Cornwallis clapped his hands. "Alright, let's rollout."

In the parking lot, Ashton ran a critical finger across Zelda's hood. "Does this thing even run?"

"Usually." So, she had a few years on her, but Zelda was still a sports car. She zoomed from zero to sixty in... really fast.

"Whatever." Ashton folded long legs into the passenger seat.

I scooted my chair and lowered the mirrors from Lois' turn behind the wheel. "Are you clear on the plan?"

"I'm capable of staying on script. I can cry on command if the situation calls for it."

"We'll play it by ear." From the hub where Cornwallis and the cops set up, Paul's house was only a few blocks.

When we arrived, Ashton rang the bell. She threw her arms around Paul, already hamming up the scene. "I'm glad you're back home, I heard the police brought you in for questioning too."

His cheeks reddened. "Nothing I couldn't handle. I made the cops chase their tails. Wait, what do you mean too?"

I followed them inside and closed the door. "Ashton endured another round of questions. Only a matter of time until they arrest her."

"On what grounds? She isn't a killer."

"Thank you. I think you're one of the few people who believe my innocence." Ashton flicked a stray tear.

"In addition to DNA, the police matched Ashton's fingerprints to a partial found on the scene. Some kind of charm or keychain matching Maria's?"

"No, no. It's part of a couple's set belonging to Justin."

"They think I planted the keychain to frame him," Ashton said. "I wanted you to tell the fan club for me. Ask them to keep me in their thoughts. With a high-priced lawyer, perhaps I can strike a deal."

"This is all wrong." Paul collapsed on the sofa. "You must fight."

"If the district attorney offers a plea bargain, Ashton's taking it. If this goes to trial, she risks life." I lifted my shoulders. "What's her alternative?"

Paul gulped a glass of water. "No one on a jury would convict you."

"Many people are jealous of my fame. Maria is a prime example."

"I'm helping Ashton explore a few avenues, but unless the real killer comes forward..." I sighed. "The police are tired of the bad press. They want the case closed now."

"Well, what about Sherry? Didn't you find the logs detailing her scandal?"

My eyebrows twitched. "What logs?"

"On the set. In evidence lockup." Paul scrunched his nose. "Oops. I'm not supposed to know about those. All these lies are hard to navigate after a while." He drew a shotgun from underneath the coffee table.

Ashton screamed like an extra in a horror flick.

"Pineapple. Pineapple. Pineapple." I licked my lips. How long would the rescue take? Would he shoot first?

"Why couldn't you leave well enough alone? No one was supposed to be on set for another hour. You show up with the barking mutt and interrupt my careful planning."

"The frame job of Justin? Please. It doesn't take Nancy Drew to unravel the phony-baloney clues."

"Given sufficient time, no one would be the wiser."

"A sloppy plan, Paul."

He stabbed the gun in my direction. "Hey. Watch who you insult. I planned to return the bat to his trailer and throw the t-shirt in the hamper to mix with his DNA. But cops crawled all over the scene forcing me to stash everything in a secondary location. Which still worked until you started snooping and accusing everyone."

"Don't blame me for sloppy work. You rushed your murder plan, plain and simple. You wanted Maria off the show allowing Ashton to steal the spotlight."

"What? That's all?" Ashton croaked. "Are you crazy?"

"Of course not." He cocked the shotgun. "Don't fill her head with lies. I'm not insane and I planned this carefully for three years. Ever since Maria locked me out of her life. We shared an incredibly close relationship but Maria slammed the door when she hit primetime. She got a restraining order on me, told the judge I stalked her. She disappeared from my life so I focused on someone new. Better. But she still found her way into my world. The things she said about you, Ashton, aren't right. I couldn't let her continue to ruin your career. I protect you because I love you."

Yeah, totally not a loon. "What about your mom, Paul? Did she assist you?"

"Leave my mother out of this."

"Did she help cover for you, after the fact?" I asked.

"She tried to support me. Same as always. She did nothing wrong." He adjusted his glasses, the grip on the shotgun loosening.

A flash of blue drifted by the window. The cavalry. But would they bust in with us at gunpoint? Would Paul shoot? "We read the text messages to your mother. You lied to her and called the murder an accident. She isn't aware of the three years of planning, is she?"

"No. It would wreck her."

"At trial, the truth will come out. Do you want to put her through the pain?" I asked.

"I don't want to hurt my mother."

"Paul, you can save Ashton and Phyllis. This is your chance to be the hero. The police are on their way here. If they catch you holding us hostage with the gun, they won't listen to your side of the story. They'll assume your mother and Ashton are instrumental in the crime."

"How?"

I cleared my throat, buying time for an explanation. "Motive. With Maria gone, she becomes a star. They can say the early morning fight was bait to lure Maria to the set where you took her life."

"Not true. I acted alone. I killed Maria Sinclair. My mother only helped hide the truth."

"Give me the shotgun and surrender yourself to the police."

"Please, Paul," Ashton added.

He tossed me the firearm, kneeled, and interlocked his fingers. I unloaded the weapon. "Pineapple? Is this thing on?"

The door splintered despite being unlocked. Cornwallis barreled inside and slapped the cuffs on Paul Marcus. "Top-notch work, Roberson."

"Thanks, CornWILBERT."

His brow crinkled at the mistake, but he didn't push. "We got a nice cushy cell for you downtown, my friend."

Ashton released a deep sigh. "I need a vacation."

"What about *Prime Suspect*?" I asked.

"You think filming will resume after this fiasco?"

"A real-life murder plot is ratings gold. Your producers won't miss their chance."

"I wouldn't bet on it." Ashton marched outside and requested an officer take her home.

"Quite the performance, Ms. Streep." Justin entered the living room with a round of applause.

I rolled my eyes. "I prefer Hepburn, more Oscars."

"Which one?" Lois asked.

"Katherine of course." My legs wobbled and I took a seat on the coffee table. "I'm glad this is over."

"We made an unbeatable team."

"Next time one of you girls is accused of murder, give me a call." Justin produced his Dodgers cap from the pocket of his jacket.

Cornwallis poked his head inside. "We need you guys at the station for debriefing. Should I assign an officer to drive you?"

"I brought my car. We'll be right behind you." I combed through my hair. Frizzy and fried, like my nerves.

"Why don't I take the wheel. You are exhausted." Justin extended his palm.

Lois placed her hands on her hips. "Why you? I'm plenty capable."

"Because Mr. Stunt Driver Man can't stand riding shotgun. Every other driver is either too slow or too fast for his taste."

"They're never too fast." Justin winked and snagged the keys. "So, what's the verdict, is Paul crazy?"

"He is clearly missing a few puzzle pieces, but his motive is deeper than pure insanity." As I climbed into the passenger seat, I gathered my thoughts. "He craves the love of the women in his life. His mother, Ashton, and Maria until a few years ago. When she filed the restraining order and moved on with her life, Paul was hurt. Jealous. When she waged war with Ashton, he felt dutybound to become the protector. To save her career."

Justin tossed his shoulder. "Sounds crazy to me."

"Hope the judge doesn't agree and let him off on an insanity defense," Lois said.

I closed my eyes as we drove to the station. After weeks of investigating, my mind finally relaxed. A poke at my elbow interrupted the catnap. "What?"

"The Dodge Charger behind us, whipping in and out of traffic."

I twisted in my seat. "I see them. So?"

"Lots of maniac drivers in L.A.," Lois added.

Justin adjusted his mirror. "Doesn't this one ring a bell?"

The obstructed plates drew my eye. "New window, crushed front fender with specks of cement."

"Is this the car responsible for running you down in the parking garage?" Lois gasped. "I figured Paul was behind the attempt?"

The car weaved through traffic, closing the gap. "Maybe Phyllis is more involved than we realized."

Lois tightened her seatbelt. "Why chase us now?"

"Because a boy's best friend is his mother." The soundtrack from *Psycho* played in my mind. "I better call Corny."

"Hold on." Justin punched the gas, accelerating down the highway.

"We don't need to cause a high-speed pursuit." Lois closed her eyes.

"She might try to run us off the road. Our best chance is to outpace her. Let's test Zelda's mettle." The Nissan Z darted in and out of traffic, making moves for a better position like Dale Earnhardt.

On the third attempt, Cornwallis answered. "Where are you guys?"

"Phyllis Montoya is chasing us."

"Are you sure?"

"Who else would be? We arrested her son after tricking him into a confession."

"Hang tight. I'll get some unies out there to cut her off."

I curled a piece of hair behind my ear. "In the meantime, we what?"

"Drive like nothing is wrong. Don't let her know you know she's in pursuit."

"Hypothetically, what if the cat's out of the bag?"

The engine revved as Justin zoomed down the fast lane. He jerked to the right and back to the left, nearly swiping other drivers. Horns honked as we flew down the highway like a couple of street racers.

"What's all the noise? Listen a chase on the highway puts everyone in danger. Pull off," Cornwallis said.

"I hear him." Justin cut across four lanes of traffic and bounced down the exit ramp.

Slower to react, Phyllis slashed through the grassy shoulder. Mud spun as she maneuvered to the road.

Lois stared out the back window. "What is she hoping to accomplish with this?"

"She probably isn't aware of Paul's confession. Or she's trying to bust him out. Who knows?"

"Cruisers are coming to you," Cornwallis said. "Don't do anything stupid."

Tires screeched as the Z whipped to a side street. We sped through the warehouse district. "Fewer cars down here." Justin fishtailed into a turn. "We'll keep her busy until the cops arrive."

We accelerated into a sharp left, barely cutting the corner. Phyllis followed and sideswiped a parked car. The jolt knocked her off course and sailing by the street. In a puff of smoke, she reversed and continued the chase. The woman must be a stunt driver in a previous career. Everyone in Hollywood dabbled in showbiz.

I hung up the phone to avoid Cornwallis' scolding. "Any ideas?"

"What about the move police do to cut off a suspect?" Lois directed the action with hand signals and an *'errrtttt'* sound effect.

"Not bad." Justin tapped the brakes and slowed to under fifty. The Charger closed the gap. "Hang tight."

"Would you like me to take the wheel so you can climb on the roof and dive on her vehicle?" I asked.

Justin chuckled. "Not this time."

Lois sighed. "I love inside jokes. Not so much when I'm locked outside, though."

We crested a hill and my stomach plummeted to my toes like a rollercoaster ride. On the descent, all four tires lifted from the ground before smacking back to earth. Phyllis stuck the landing with far less skill. Her hubcap rolled down the street, a casualty of the chase.

Justin pumped the brakes until our vehicles rode parallel-. "Suddenly I'm a flyweight picking a fight with a heavyweight."

I flashed my best 'Lucy face'. "Physics. We're in the little car. Will the bump maneuver work?"

"If I'm careful." Justin jerked the wheel and nudged the bumper. The Charger fishtailed but stayed on course. He attempted a second shove. Wheels spun, pushing Phyllis into the other lane. The Z looped, braking into a turn and blocking an escape route. An overcorrection sent Phyllis headfirst into a telephone pole.

We spilled from the car and approached the accident with care. Lois twisted her neck. "Is she alive?"

Phyllis fell to the ground with a gash on her forehead. "What did you do to my son?"

"Nothing. He confessed." I checked over my shoulder as sirens dotted the horizon, mixing with the setting sun. "The police are here so don't try anything."

"What can I possibly try?" She swatted hair from her face. "I'm ruined, right?"

"We read your text messages," Lois said.

"Why did you cover for your son after everything he did? Why did you attempt to kill us?"

"I wanted to scare you is all." Phyllis clutched a hand to her heart. "He didn't mean to hurt Maria. His rage overpowers him sometimes. They fought and he hit her once. He panicked when he realized what happened."

Justin scoffed. "He lied, lady."

27

That's a Wrap

Lois paced by the door. "Becky! Come on, we're going to be late." She checked the time. "This is our chance to make a better second, first impression."

I tapped Lorelai's bowl. "It's yummy dog food. Please eat." I stretched for the cookie jar and threw a biscuit in the mix. "I spy a treat on top." Lorelai chomped the cookie and wagged her tail for another one. "Man, she really hates her Kibble."

"She's betting you'll cave and add something special if she waits you out."

"An evil genius." Despite the words, I used a baby-talk voice. Never thought I would be *that* kind of pet owner.

I snagged my purse and tied my shoes. "I'm ready."

"Say it."

I flashed a 'scout's honor' signal after first attempting and correcting the *Star Trek* sign. "I promise if I discover a body on the set, I will not touch it, I will not drop evidence on the scene, and I will not get involved."

"I don't believe you but I don't want to waste time arguing." Lois jerked her neck flipping her long locks into my face. "Speaking of which, did Paul plant your keycard under the body to throw suspicion?"

"Apparently the frame job is all my clumsy doing. I moved Maria when I searched for a pulse and snagged the badge on her clothing. Who knew?"

Lois rolled her eyes. "If not for your flub, Justin might be behind bars right now, so that's something."

After a painless drive, we arrived on the set. Lois proceeded through security without a second glance. But Pebble stopped and rubbed his head as if the goose egg recognized me. "You!"

I offered a sheepish shrug. "No hard feelings for the frying pan to the noggin? I was hunting a murderer."

"This is the thug who knocked you out?" The other guard rolled back in his office chair. "Some burly street gang leader? She's a little girl."

"I'm stronger than I look." I waved to the gate. "May I go?"

Pebble waved me through. "Lucky shot."

We entered the staff meeting right on time. Justin motioned to the saved seats. "I decided to slum it back here with the stagehands today."

I looped my purse on the back of the chair. "Don't do us any favors."

"Truth is I can't stand to share a row with Ashton Ashley. She's telling everyone about her takedown of Paul and the integral role she played."

"I may not care for her but we don't secure a confession from Paul without her," Lois said.

Justin hissed. "Shh. She might hear you."

Sherry Newton entered the conference room with reading glasses perched on her nose. I gulped, wondering if she held a grudge. "How did she keep her job after all the leaking to the killer's mother?"

"Producers are sweeping everything else under the rug," Justin whispered. "Scandal doesn't help our ratings but the murder biz does. I'm thankful for a gig."

"Your chance at stardom."

"Good morning everyone." Sherry settled the crowd. "I am pleased to say we are back to full capacity and filming will begin this afternoon."

A round of cheers erupted.

"A heartfelt thanks to the people who caught Maria's killer. Not an easy task and a lot of people were wrong with their accusations." Sherry removed her glasses and locked eyes with me. "Justin Woods, Lois Vo, and Becky ROBINSON you saved our show."

I couldn't hide the grin. I didn't catch my big break in Hollywood but at least someone finally got my name right.

Ashton raised her hand. "Me too! I helped."

"Excellent point. Thank you for bringing it to my attention. Ashton played a vital role in apprehending the murderer, who happened to be the president of her fan club." Sherry applauded. "Well done."

After handing out assignments, Sherry dismissed the meeting. I glared at my latest placement with the sound department. What did an assistant sound person do? Hold a boom mic or calling for quiet on the set?

Justin snagged my hand and pulled me aside. "I don't want to get you in trouble with the Dragon Lady but can you spare a second?"

"Sure."

"I want to thank you."

I waved off the rest of his statement. "You already did."

"Not properly." He tugged on his Dodgers cap, giving me memories of our first meeting. Before I realized a movie star hid beneath the hat.

I smiled at the thought of my broken shoe and the save from Prince Charming. If we worked on a Hallmark movie, people might call it a 'meet cute moment'. But we didn't and it wasn't.

Even if he wasn't getting over the murder of his ex-girlfriend, why would the Hollywood Hunk give the small-town girl a second look? Wasn't that a standard romcom plot?

I shook the notion and realized I stopped listening. "I'm sorry, what did you say?"

He twitched into a half-grin. "You trusted me when I looked guilty, and you cleared my name. I want to repay the favor."

"I don't plan on becoming a murder suspect a second time just so you can prove my innocence."

"So literal." He rocked on his heels. "I gave your name to a casting agent friend of mine. She'll be on the lookout for commercial work if you're interested."

"You're amazing... I mean that's amazing. Not that you aren't too but specifically the name, agent, commercial aspect." I took a deep breath and counted backward from three to stop the gibberish. "Thank you."

"One phone call with no promise of a role hardly makes us even.-But it's a start." He winked.

"Becky, we're going to be late." Lois' interruption allowed me to cover my blushing cheeks.

"Coming."

"I'm off to wardrobe." Justin saluted. "See you guys around the next crime scene."

Lois and I strolled outside into the fresh air. An amused glint sparkled in her eyes. "What is that about?"

"What?"

"You're secret conversation with Dodger Boy."

"He thanked me for clearing his name."

"He must be mailing me a card." Lois crossed her arms. "That wasn't about a thank you."

"What then?"

"You're going to pretend Justin isn't your Hollywood crush?"

"Things are different when you meet in real life." I shrugged. "We're friends."

"Uh-huh."

I ignored her insinuation and navigated the phony New York alleyway. For the first time since being hired, we enjoyed wandering a backlot. I leaned on a cardboard cutout of a famous action star. "Maybe the rebooted show will be different. We're on the way to the top, Lo Vo. I can feel it." I motioned for her to snap a picture. But my gyrations knocked the movie star's head clean off his cardboard body.

Lois slapped her forehead. "Might take longer than we originally thought."

Forget acting lessons, did anyone offer classes to combat klutzy behavior and dumb luck?

Ready for Becky's next Hollywood adventure?
Continue reading for a sneak peek.

Order Now

Dear Readers

Thank you for reading PRIME TIME MURDER. I hope you enjoyed the book and are looking forward to the sequel STAND-IN MURDER.

Curious how Becky ended up in Hollywood?

DOWNLOAD THE FREE SHORT STORY TODAY!
www.brittanybrinegar.com/subscribe

I love hearing from readers. If you have a moment, please leave a review online and let me know what you thought.

About the Author

Brittany E. Brinegar is the author of witty mysteries and whodunits. When you open one of her books, look out for rapid-fire banter and nostalgic pop culture references.

Her hobbies include time travel to the 1940s, solving mysteries, and training to be a super spy... vicariously through her characters of course.

She lives in Arlington, Texas with two canine writing companions/distractions and loves drawing inspiration from family, friends, and her home state.

Ready to smile your way through murder? Join Brittany's newsletter and never miss a new release.

Website: https://www.brittanybrinegar.com/

Explore the Lake Falls Universe

If you enjoyed this series and are interested in more, take a deeper dive into the Lake Falls universe. All my mysteries, historical and cozy alike, take place in the same world. In fact, you'll notice several connections between the series, including a family resemblance. Explore my website for more details and character connections.

Small-Town Girl

Stand-In Murder: Sneak Peek

I repeated my mantra as I entered the mundane office building. *Inhale confidence, exhale doubt.* Positive thinking, self-love mumbo jumbo but at least it reminded me to breathe.

At the entrance, I reread the casting call. Before I announced my presence at reception, I wanted to make sure the role suited me.

Monica (Female 20-25) is a small-town girl from the South. She moved to the big city after inheriting her estranged grandmother's inn.

The generic description fit perfectly and open calls meant a nobody like me might wow the casting director. But what kind of chance did I have at a lead role? My eyes scanned the competition. Full room, even for an independent film offering little pay.

My heart thumped as I compared my wardrobe choices to the other ladies. They looked like the casting call for *Devil Wears Prada*. My choice of jeans, a cute top, and minimal makeup might as well be overalls and a straw hat in comparison.

Putting on blinders, I scanned the script the receptionist provided. Corny dialogue, predictable storyline, tragic ending. I sighed, knowing I couldn't afford to be picky. Hollywood agents didn't beat down my door to sign me.

The casting director made a brief announcement and summoned the first girl. Somehow, I forgot the movie standard for the girl-next-door type – supermodel with glasses to obscure her beauty.

I leaned to the actress beside me. "Aren't you in the Geico commercial?"

"Shh. I'm trying to read this before they call me. Bother somebody else."

No wonder the serial killer located her hiding spot with such ease. She wasn't the sharpest chainsaw in the shed.

The front door swung open, bouncing the Venetian blinds. A woman with her hair piled in a messy bun, sweats, and Uggs bustled to reception. She slung sunglasses through her reddish-blonde roots and smacked gum as she signed in.

I twisted my head, recognition flooding. She was one of the blondies from the country club – Strawberry. I ran across her during the Maria Sinclair murder investigation.

She plopped into the chair next to me. "I know you, right?"

"Yeah. We played suspects for Agent Cornwallis."

Strawberry flashed dimples. "I remember you saved the day. I'm Vicky Berryhill."

"Becky Robinson." I pointed to my chest. "I'm glad I'm not the only one here without a subscription to Saks Fifth Avenue."

"These stuffy, uptight ones usually land the role. Directors figure they can dress someone down but they can't do much for an ugly duckling."

"Shh!" over officious Geico Girl hissed.

Vicky's eyes widened and she spread her arms. "If you want quiet study time, go to the library." She rolled her dark blue eyes. "These people need to lighten up."

"Can I ask about your ensemble, Vicky?"

"Well, I can dress exactly like thirty other girls, or I can be memorable." She grinned. "I tried the other way. Never experienced much luck with callbacks."

"We reached a similar conclusion." I waved a hand over my outfit. "Not like the other option is within my price range."

"You're new to the business, aren't you?"

My eyes crossed. "Did I forget to remove the rookie stamp from my forehead again?"

"You're too wholesome for this industry, Becky. You'll never make it."

I filled the silence with nervous laughter. How did someone respond to such an incredulous claim? "You never can tell. Perhaps my charming personality will play right into the director's hand."

"Hey, don't be insulted by my bluntness. I hung around this life for a long time. You're from some no-name Nebraska town where you excelled on the tiny stage. People from the surrounding counties talked about your sure rise to fame. You made the move, live in a dump, and barely make ends meet."

"Sounds like an autobiography."

She cackled, despite the intended insult. Maybe I was too saccharine. "Might be my story if I didn't marry up. Didn't do squat for my acting career but at least my roof doesn't leak."

"Is your husband in the business?"

"A writer. Situational comedies and a few plays."

"Nothing major for him either? So, what makes you the expert?"

"Success is relative out here. One minute you're hot, the next you're yesterday's news." She closed one eye. "I like you though, Becky. You have..."

"Spunk?"

"No. I'm thinking more along the line of manners." She huffed. "But you would benefit from some pluck. It may develop over time."

"Are you trying to psych out the competition?"

"Sweetie, if that is the case, I would talk to Miss Tennessee over there." She adjusted her messy bun. "I admire you for taking the plunge but first auditions are disastrous. If you remember your name, you're ahead of the game."

"Perhaps IQ factors into the name thing."

"How about spunky in training?" She took a swig of green tea. "Since you're such a good sport, I'll do one thing to help you out."

"Which is?"

She reached inside her oversized bag and produced a business card. "No one will take you seriously without an agent. This is mine. Give him a call. He doesn't solicit new clients but he owes me a favor."

Flip Warner? A Hollywood name if I ever heard one. I rubbed the cardstock between my fingers, unsure if I should accept. The entire conversation with the woman confused me.

"I'm up next. Try not to throw up in front of the panel."

My stomach vaulted on command, wracked with nerves. "Thanks, but I'm not worried."

She pointed a thumb at the audition area as she left. "Hope you're more believable in the room."

Geico Girl leaned over and whispered. "She's a piece of work."

I squashed the fierce temptation to shush her back since my personality forbade such cruelty. "Who made Vicky the authority? Self-appointed?"

"She's as far from a breakthrough as the rest of us," Geico Girl said. "But the difference is, she hangs around a ritzy crowd and thinks she's above us. Somebody should knock her off the high horse."

The clock on the wall ticked by at an agonizing pace. With the last name Robinson, my turn didn't come until the bottom of the list. The point in the audition process where the casting directors already chose a favorite and became annoyed by all the talentless hacks wasting their time.

I handed my resume to the man at the end of the table. He passed it down the line to the others. Printing one copy - rookie mistake.

Each person took a few minutes to skim the paper. The more I studied them, the more I fixated on the resemblance to the original *American Idol* judges. Almost dead ringers.

As I stood in front of the panel, my anxiety multiplied. My eyes found my shoes and I wished I wore the ruby slippers. Three clicks to blink home. I attempted to quiet my fidgeting but the hyperawareness caused a chain reaction of ticks. Strawberry's words reverberated in my head.

"Do you sing or dance?" the Simon Cowell character asked.

I swallowed the sandpaper clogging my voice. "The flyer didn't call for any talent in music."

"But you left the section blank on the sign-in sheet."

I cleared my throat. "Tone deaf and two left feet. This isn't a musical is it?"

Paula Abdul raised her hand. "I'm impressed by this president of the Lake Falls Theatrical Society. Where is this?"

"My high school in Lake Falls, Texas."

"Oh."

"You are from the South though?" Randy asked.

"Texas."

He adjusted his glasses. "Accent doesn't sound authentic. Are you putting something on to impress us?"

"No this is my normal drawl. Born and raised."

Simon clicked his tongue. "The girl from New Hampshire did it better."

Paula pushed his arm. "Well, it won't hurt to allow her to do the scene. She's waited this long."

"If we must," Simon shrugged.

The audition was doomed to fail from the start. Less than a page in, Simon gave the stop signal, "Enough."

They offered the obligatory *thanks for coming down, we'll be in touch*. But I didn't hold my breath.

As I left the audition, I wondered if Strawberry landed the part.- Turned out she had bigger concerns, like being murdered.

Order ***Stand-In Murder*** Today!

Order Now

Also By

Hollywood Whodunit

A Humorous Cozy Mystery

Prime Time Murder (Book 1)
Her mother warned her about crime in the big city. But Becky Robinson chased her Hollywood dream anyway. Now the police think she murdered a movie star.

Stand-In Murder (Book 2)
When a struggling actress turns up dead the police are eager to rule suicide. It's up to Becky and Lois to prove the police wrong before the killer makes his next move.

Music City Murder (Book 3)
When Becky's cousin is accused of murder, the gang travels to Nashville to clear her name.

Trap Door Murder (Book 4)
When the headliner dies in the middle of his Las Vegas magic show, it's up to Becky to solve his murder.

Fool's Gold Murder (Book 5)
The gang heads north to gold country to film the pilot of a western TV show. But things go awry when a curious puppy unearths a skeleton and a treasure map.

Holly Jolly Murder (Book 6)
It's Christmas in Hollywood. Get ready for fake snow, a publicity stunt, and real murder.

Blue Suede Murder (Book 7)
When Becky is roped into a family cruise with her divorced parents, she hopes for a distraction. So of course, there's a murder.

Robinson Family Detective Agency

A Humorous Cozy Mystery

Red Herrings & Pink Flamingos

McGuffins & Birdies

A Hoax & a Hex

A Patsy & a Pastry

A Trick & a Pony

A Masterpiece & a Murder

Spies of Texas

A Witty Historical Mystery

Enigma of Lake Falls **(Book 1)**
When rumors of a Russian spy turn Lake Falls upside down, Sawyer and Jenny embark on a treacherous journey for the truth. In a town with more secrets than people, everyone is a suspect.

Undercover Pursuit **(Book 2)**
Sawyer and Jenny head to Boston to investigate her mysterious past. While searching for answers, they fall into a world of corruption and Irish mobsters.

Cloak & Danger **(Book 3)**
The third installment in the Spies of Texas series follows Jenny and Sawyer on their first sanctioned mission. Follow the pair to the slopes of Lake Tahoe as they hunt a missing spy.

Anthologies

Made in the USA
Las Vegas, NV
19 November 2022

59789249R10125